"W

One of the men moved in front of the lamp. He was short, scrawny, and his slicked-down hair shone in the lamplight. The term grease ball came to mind immediately. He smiled a now-I've-got-you-where-I-want-you smile and said, "You ain't bad-looking for such a big girl."

Maggie's heart stopped when his sweaty fingers lifted her chin. "You just answer our questions, sweetmeat," he promised in a gritty voice, "and I'll go easy on you when all of this is over." The weasel then backed into line with his cohorts.

Tucker felt an unexpected sense of repugnance, and when the man touched Maggie, something snapped inside him. Despite the odds against him, he was barely able to hold himself back. That worried him. He was a trained professional with a job to do. Why, then, did he have to keep reminding himself of that?

Dear Reader,

Welcome to Silhouette. Experience the magic of the wonderful world where two people fall in love. Meet heroines who will make you cheer for their happiness, and heroes (be they the boy next door or a handsome, mysterious stranger) who will win your heart. Silhouette Romances reflect the magic of love—sweeping you away with books that will make you laugh and cry, heartwarming, poignant stories that will move you time and time again.

In the next few months, we're publishing romances by many of your all-time favorites, such as Diana Palmer, Brittany Young, Emilie Richards and Arlene James. Your response to these authors and other authors of Silhouette Romances has served as a touchstone for us, and we're pleased to bring you more books with Silhouette's distinctive medley of charm, wit and—above all—*romance*.

I hope you enjoy this book and the many stories to come. Experience the magic!

Sincerely,

Tara Hughes
Senior Editor
Silhouette Books

PEPPER
ADAMS

In Hot Pursuit

Silhouette Romance
Published by Silhouette Books New York
America's Publisher of Contemporary Romance

To our teacher, Bonnie,
for leading us into temptation.

SILHOUETTE BOOKS
300 E. 42nd St., New York, N.Y. 10017

ISBN: 0-373-08504-4

First Silhouette Books printing May 1987

America's Publisher of Contemporary Romance

Printed in the U.S.A.

Books by Pepper Adams

Silhouette Romance

Heavenly Bodies #486
In Hot Pursuit #504

PEPPER ADAMS

lives in Oklahoma with her husband and children. Her interest in romance writing began with obsessive reading and was followed by courses where she learned the craft. She longs for the discipline of the "rigid schedule" all the how-to books exhort writers to maintain, but does not really believe she will achieve it in this lifetime. She finds she works best if she remembers to take her writing seriously but not herself.

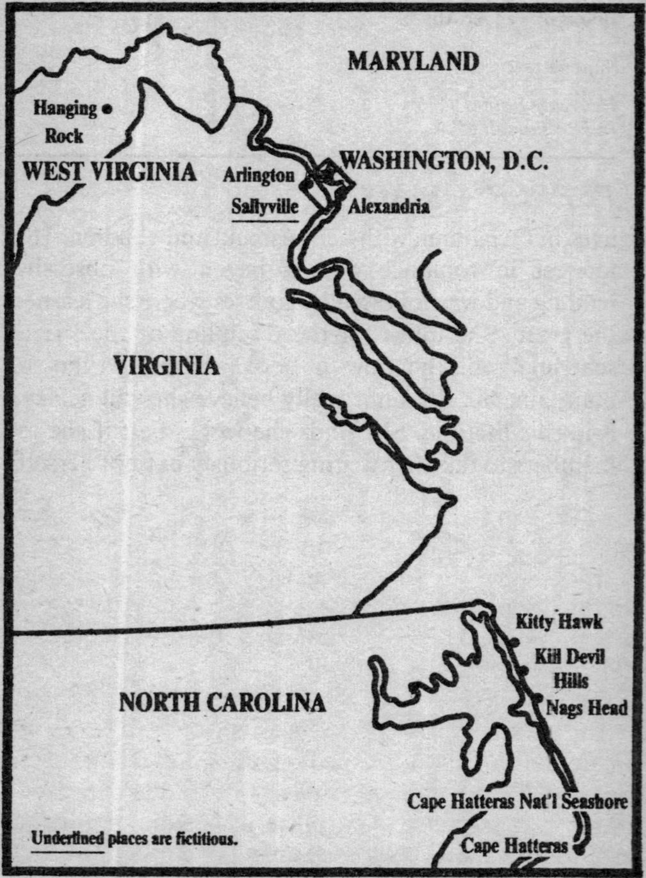
MARYLAND
Hanging Rock
WEST VIRGINIA
Arlington
WASHINGTON, D.C.
Sallyville
Alexandria
VIRGINIA
Kitty Hawk
Kill Devil Hills
Nags Head
NORTH CAROLINA
Cape Hatteras Nat'l Seashore
Underlined places are fictitious.
Cape Hatteras

Chapter One

Who would have believed it? Maggie Ryan—cruising for men!

In the two weeks she'd been under J. P. Tucker's surveillance no men had come courting Miss Mousey. And according to the guys in wiretap they weren't exactly burning up the phone lines, either. Apparently Ms. Ryan had never heard that blondes were supposed to have more fun. She didn't seem to have any at all.

Until tonight.

Tucker's seasoned glance took in the noisy club whose ultramodern decor depended on mirrors and flashing lights for warmth. He'd been in plenty of places like this. Too many. It was the kind of place where the desirability of members of the opposite sex grew the closer it got to closing time.

Everyone came for the same reason. To meet someone. The burning question on Tucker's mind tonight was, who had Maggie Ryan come here to meet? He'd tailed the two blond young women discreetly all the way from Sallyville to

Arlington and had been more than surprised when they'd pulled into the parking lot of Tingle's. He knew the notorious singles' bar was the in spot of the area. He knew it was where young GS 5s and GS 7s came to see and be seen. What he didn't know was what Maggie Ryan was doing there.

Tucker stationed himself in a seat near the door, where he had a clear view of the subject's table. Being the conscientious public servant that he was, he ordered a ginger ale from the good-looking waitress and totally resented the fact that he was on duty. That was a come-hither look she'd given him if he'd ever seen one, and she looked like his kind of woman.

Body by Fisher. Brain by Mattel.

"How do you like it?" Holly cupped her mouth with her hands as though Maggie were on the next mountaintop instead of sitting across the tiny table.

"It's kind of noisy, isn't it?" Maggie yelled back.

"Not when you're dancing." Holly frowned, then added, "Why aren't you dancing with any of the guys who've asked you?"

"I don't dance outside my species?" She thought of her last partner, a little creep who'd actually had the nerve to nuzzle her bosom on the dance floor. Granted, he was awfully short, but he could have craned his neck a bit for propriety's sake. She'd made up her mind to reject any future offers.

For the past hour she had sipped Chablis and sat watching the room, wishing she was home with a good book. Holly wriggled hips with anyone who asked and returned to the table only for brief intervals. No doubt she felt guilty for having insisted that Maggie come along.

It had gotten to the point that Maggie, merely by looking at the man, could determine which of them was about to be invited to trip the light fantastic. If he was tall, blemish free and had all his own hair, he was Holly's.

"I told you to wear something foxy," Holly hissed.

"I'm not sure I *own* anything foxy." Maggie shrugged. "Define the term, will you?"

Holly surveyed her friend's attire thoughtfully. "Well, in your case, anything with a waist. I don't know where you manage to find all those baggy sweaters."

"I knit them," she retorted.

"Sorry. Do me a favor and get me a subscription to Hunk-of-the-Month for Christmas, huh?"

"Very funny." Maggie gave Holly a cynical smile. "This little outing wasn't my idea. I still don't know why we had to drive all the way into Arlington just to go to a singles' bar."

"Because Sallyville doesn't have a singles' bar."

"I knew there was a reason I liked that town," Maggie mumbled. To Holly she said, "But it's so late."

"Take my word for it, Maggie, it wouldn't have been nearly this much fun if we'd come in the morning."

Maggie made a face at her friend's retreating back as Holly rejoined the dancing throng, led by a handsome blond man. "Ain't we got fun," she muttered under her breath.

She would never understand why Holly McGinley wanted to be her friend. They had absolutely nothing in common. Although Maggie enjoyed quiet evenings at home, Holly claimed solitude made her climb the walls. Holly was a bright social butterfly who attracted men in droves, while Maggie had no experience at all.

Physically, they weren't so unalike, but whereas Holly had parlayed her tall, coltish blond looks into glamorous excess, Maggie had opted for inconspicuousness. Her own hair was a shade of blond that looked as if it had planned to be brown but changed its mind at the last minute. Her driver's license listed the color of her eyes as green, but sometimes they were almost brown—depending on her mood.

And as for her height, at five-eight she had never grown completely comfortable in her skin. Maggie was certain she was really a petite person trying to navigate a lanky body. She felt she had all the grace of a little girl trying to walk in her mother's high heels. Her own mother insisted it was merely an awkward stage she would eventually outgrow. At twenty-five, Maggie was no longer optimistic.

This was not the fun-filled evening she had been promised, and Maggie wondered why Holly had insisted on dragging her along. Maybe because she was one of the few people Holly knew who was sure not to have plans on a Friday night. The more she thought about it, the more she realized that Holly needed someone. It would appear far too predatory to walk into a place like this alone. It was much better to be accompanied by another female. A nonthreatening, invisible female. Less competition that way.

"Excuse me," someone said at her elbow. "Dance?"

She'd entertained herself devising categories for the men who approached her. This one was too anxious and he had his hands behind his back, probably rubbing his sweaty palms. Too bad his parents hadn't sought orthodontia. For all she knew he could be a regular Boy Scout, but Maggie wasn't about to risk being groped again to find out.

"No, thank you," she answered, smiling sweetly. "I'm contemplating suicide at the moment. I think I'll just sit this one out."

"Sure, okay. Certainly." He gave her a weird look and beat a hasty retreat. No doubt spreading the word that the dishwater blonde in the unfoxy sweater was handicapped by more than just her taste in clothes.

Tucker wondered what made a woman like Maggie Ryan tick.

She clearly wasn't there to dance. Men approached her but she seemed determined to remain a wallflower. Was she about to make a contact?

It just didn't figure. She was about as unlikely a counterfeiter as he ever hoped to find. No one from Ekalaka,

Montana, could possibly be mixed up with the gang the department was after. He'd tried telling that to Peterson, but his superior had insisted that anyone even remotely connected with Haversham Photography was suspect and should be under surveillance. Ms. Ryan worked for Haversham, and it was Tucker's unfortunate luck to have been assigned to follow her around.

Haversham. Now there was a suspect. But in his infinite wisdom, Peterson had assigned a rookie to tail him. There was no justice in the world. Burl Haversham had spent over eighteen months in a prison cell with Jiggs Skirby. Skirby was known to be in Mexico violating his parole and an informant had reported that the ex-con had designs for almost perfect counterfeit hundred-dollar-bill plates. The department suspected the plans had been smuggled into the U.S. to an unknown accomplice. Haversham?

Or Maggie Ryan?

Right. She was a real dangerous criminal, a mouse in a world of lions. He knew everything about her since he'd had plenty of time to study her short, uninteresting dossier. Every night it was the same old humdrum affair. She went straight home after work and her lights were always out by 10:30 p.m. Except last Saturday night when she had thrown caution to the wind and stayed up until midnight working on some god-awful lump of a thing.

Tucker had always been a leg man, so he couldn't help noticing that Maggie had great-looking legs. She wasn't bad looking; in fact, she reminded him of one of those "before" pictures in magazines. Tonight she was more of an "after," bordering on beautiful. But what was with all those shapeless skirts and baggy sweaters she wore? Was she trying to hide some terrible figure flaw?

He was sorely tempted to find out.

What better way to satisfy his curiosity about her oversize clothing and what it concealed than to ask her to dance? But it appeared she was picky. Or perhaps selective, depending on which side of the rejection you happened to be on. Since women rarely turned him down for anything, Tucker itched to try out his charms on the uncharmable Ms. Ryan.

But that would be bad form. He was a Secret Service agent who didn't always bother to go by the book, but he'd better not. No point blowing his cover for one stupid dance.

She probably didn't know how to, anyway.

Her hyper blond friend looked like a funky model but in reality was working her way up in a bureaucratic clerical pool. In fact, her background checked out much more interestingly than Maggie's. She returned to the table, and the two heads got together over their wineglasses.

This is it, he figured. Miss Mousey is telling Ms. Golightly that it's past her bedtime, and Ms. Golightly is arguing that the fun is just getting started. He'd better watch out—he was getting good at creating these little scenarios in his mind.

That's what came of too many stakeouts.

God, he hated stakeouts. And he'd been assigned some doozies in his career with the Treasury Department—like bodyguarding the aging widows of former presidents. Until tonight he'd thought his present assignment was almost as boring and uneventful.

"Maybe I should just take a taxi, if you want to stay for a while," Maggie suggested. She had to get out of this place.

"All the way to Sallyville?"

"It isn't that far."

"It is when the meter's running. Just stay a little longer," Holly wheedled. "Loosen up. Let yourself go. Live a little. If you'd dance with some of these guys who've been asking, you'd have a good time."

Now why did Maggie doubt that? Doing singles' bars was like playing tug of war, she decided. Just one big jerk after another. She wanted to get back to her novel and find out if the detective heroine, Clementine Kent, had yet discovered that the power broker's son was the cold-blooded killer Maggie suspected him of being. Fleetingly she wondered if it was psychologically unhealthy to live life vicariously through the books she read. Probably. But it was the only chance she had for some exciting adventure.

"This racket is giving me a headache," Maggie complained.

Holly eyed her doubtfully, so Maggie arranged her features in what she hoped was a mask of pain—like an actor in an aspirin commercial.

"Go outside for a few minutes and get some fresh air." If Holly was anything she was resourceful.

Maggie didn't bother to point out that the air outside was heavy with smog and exhaust fumes. "Maybe I'll do just that."

Holly clutched her arm. "Don't look now, but that rugged, gorgeous-looking guy over by the door is staring at you again. He hasn't taken his eyes off you all evening."

Across the room, Tucker shook his head ruefully. It was a crying shame. All that marvelous femininity going to waste beneath those shapeless garments. She might as well be wearing a sign saying, Hi, I'm Repressed.

Uh-oh. He'd been caught watching her. Now Ms. Golightly was pointing at him behind her hand. She'd never heard the old saw about discretion being the better part of valor.

Maggie nonchalantly turned her head a fraction and slowly rolled her eyes in the direction indicated by Holly's half-hidden finger. She was right. He was staring. Making her voice as unaffected as possible she said, "So?"

"So? Maybe he's bashful. He probably wants to dance with you but is afraid to ask because you keep turning everyone down."

Once again Maggie's gaze swiveled in the direction of the good-looking man in question. Too bad he *hadn't* asked her to dance. She would have seriously considered just about any request he might have made. It was difficult to tell much in the dim nightclub, but he looked very nice. Kind of like a buttoned-down Indiana Jones. He didn't look as though he normally hung out in places like this, and that in itself was a recommendation.

"Why don't you go over and ask him?"

"Oh, no. I just couldn't." Could she? Suddenly Maggie's heart skipped a beat, then hammered frantically as her senses were caught up in a spider tangle of unfamiliar impulses.

"Sure you could. At least give it a try. What have you got to lose?"

What indeed? She wanted to. Oh, how she wanted to. "I don't think—"

"Don't think," Holly interrupted. "For once in your life just do something without thinking it to death."

"What would I say? What would I do?" Maggie bit her lip in indecision then voiced another, more relevant question. "What if he's short?"

"Good grief, Maggie, you aren't asking the man to father your children. Who cares? Just go over there and ask him. If it turns out he's a munchkin... well, you'll think of something."

Easy for her to say. It wasn't Holly's bosom that had been nuzzled. "I don't know. What if he turns me down?"

"Then it will be your turn to be rejected. But, Maggie, you owe it to yourself to try. Besides, I have a feeling this is going to be your lucky night."

"Okay," she sighed with all the enthusiasm Marie Antoinette must have displayed on her way to the guillotine. "I'll do it." She told herself that she was only agreeing to this madness because Holly was anxious to get back on the floor. The fact that one look at the stranger turned her knees to Jell-O had absolutely nothing to do with it.

She downed the rest of her wine and made her way toward him but stopped short when she caught sight of the sultry waitress bending over his table. It was a move clearly calculated to advertise the redhead's assets.

Tucker froze. Oh, no, he thought. Maggie was homing in on him like a bee to its hive.

Had she realized he was following her? Or was she merely attracted enough to invite him to dance? He couldn't let that happen despite his earlier musings. His cover would be blown and he'd be forced to ask for reassignment. No doubt Peterson would frown on that. Since his recent divorce, Peterson had frowned on everything.

He sighed with relief when the cocktail waitress—Gina, according to her name tag—leaned low over his table. "I've got a tip for you," she gushed suggestively. "I get off at one."

Tucker smiled apologetically. "Sorry, honey, but I've got work to do." He pulled a ten spot from his pocket and folded it. "But it just so happens, I've got a tip for you, too."

"Poor little me, with no pockets." She pouted, breathed deeply, then glanced suggestively at her own low-cut neckline.

Tucker liked his women agreeable, but this was ridiculous. However, he'd have to play along for the moment to discourage Maggie from coming any closer. It must have worked, for she stopped dead in her tracks with what seemed to be a look of wide-eyed astonishment on her face.

He felt reasonably sure his audience was captive, so he flashed Gina his never-fail grin and winked boldly. "Why don't I just put it right here next to your heart? And tonight when you're undressing it'll remind you of me."

Maggie clenched her jaw as she watched him flirt with the busty redhead. He said something and the girl laughed delightedly. Then the lecher had the audacity to stuff a wad of money into the woman's scanty, clinging top. Maggie closed her gaping mouth. Boy, sometimes first impressions sure were misleading. He'd seemed so nice sitting across the room with that out-of-place look on his face.

Maggie turned toward the exit. She was smart enough to know when she was outdistanced. That redhead had everything she didn't.

Gina giggled as Tucker poked the money into her cleavage. "Maybe next time," she cooed.

"Maybe." Never, he added silently, watching the waitress sashay to another table. She had thick ankles. Maggie's, on the other hand...

He'd taken his eyes off Maggie for only a second, and now she was nowhere in sight. She must have gone outside alone, he noted, because Ms. Golightly was still boogeying. Damning himself for his preoccupation with female anatomy, Tucker headed for the door.

Outside, Maggie noticed that winter was definitely on its way. She loved October in Virginia, with its flashy displays of autumn color and the warm days and cool nights of Indian summer. Not like Montana, where the snow was known to fly as early as September. She pulled her sweater closer. Without the warm crush of bodies to elevate the temperature, it was quite chilly. Before they got home, Holly would be wishing *she* had a baggy red sweater.

Thank goodness it was Friday. It was getting to be a strain trying to look busy all day. With business so slow, Maggie often wondered why she'd been hired at Haversham's in the first place. She assumed most of the calls that came in were personal because her boss took them in the privacy of his office. She'd been hired as a receptionist but there wasn't much to receive. Today she'd even volunteered to call names from the local directory to quote special portrait rates to the parents of small children. Everybody was a sucker when it came to having pictures of their kids. But Mr. Haversham had vetoed the idea without explanation, as though he had no desire to encourage business.

Even walk-in customers seemed to set her boss on edge. This afternoon a man had come in the studio from the alley entrance, and Mr. Haversham had nervously thrust her tote bag in her hands and told her to go on home. Half an hour early.

What a career. She hadn't spent seven years in college to while away her days rearranging paper clips in her drawer and polishing her desk with spray-on wax.

There wasn't a big demand for people with master's degrees in fine art. They were worthless in the workplace, so until she sold some of her sculptures, she had no alternative. Maggie supposed she could go into D.C. and try for a government job, but she couldn't type or run a word processor and she'd never be able to afford the inflated rents of the District, even if her parents were willing to send her a monthly check. And she'd had to move a continent away to escape their well-intentioned interference.

Besides, she liked Sallyville. It reminded her of home, and she didn't have anyone peering over her shoulder all the time. She guessed that she would always be a small-town girl at heart.

Her work might be boring and lonely, but she had her sculpture and art for fulfillment. And her reading gave her more than enough stimulating companionship. Didn't it? Lately she had toyed with the idea of getting a cat but had fought the impulse on the grounds that feline acquisition was the first step to acknowledging spinsterhood.

She noticed a green sedan parked illegally across the street. Wasn't it the same car she'd seen several times before, parked outside Haversham's, across from her apartment building, and once in the library parking lot? If she were the heroine in one of the mysteries she was always reading, she would swear she was being followed. But that was absurd. Why would anyone waste his time following a struggling sculptress who rearranged paper clips for her daily bread?

Maggie turned at the end of the block and headed back to Tingle's. She forgot about the sedan as her mind drifted to more serious matters, like the novel she'd been reading. She couldn't wait to get back to *Murder in the Boardroom* and find out if Clementine had discovered who was killing off all those corporate executives.

Maggie was eager for this dull evening to be over, eager to be caught up in the world of make-believe. She wanted to experience the emotion, the excitement that Clementine knew. She wanted to feel as if it were all happening to her.

She smiled in anticipation. The next thing she knew someone grabbed her right arm, twisted it painfully behind her back and clapped a rough arm around her ribs. It took several seconds for the significance of the action to penetrate Maggie's stunned brain.

She was being attacked.

Scream, her brain demanded when it finally kicked into gear. But when she opened her mouth, no sound emerged. It was like a horrible, terrifying nightmare in which she tried and tried to call for help—but couldn't. Only this was no nightmare. This was really happening.

And it was happening to *her.*

"Just keep quiet and you won't get hurt," a deep voice growled in her ear.

What else could she do? Fight? Fighting was pretty academic at this point; her arm felt as though it were imprisoned by a steel band.

Flee? How could she even think about running when she was being held in a vise?

Screaming was out. Her vocal cords had betrayed her and refused to function. Even if she was able to squeak a sound, who would hear? The pounding music from the club filled the air, and there was no one on the street. No one but Maggie Ryan and her mugger.

A car braked at the curb, the back door flew open and she was stuffed unceremoniously inside. Another man, of equal stature and just as unsavory looking as her attacker, hunched behind the wheel. Wait a minute—muggers did not provide transportation.

A strangling dread tightened Maggie's throat, and her teeth began to chatter. Why hadn't she stayed home with her novel tonight? It was far preferable to read about crime than to experience it firsthand.

"Oh damn!" The concrete was barely under Tucker's feet when he spotted Maggie being shoved into the back seat of a late-model Caprice. He raced to his green LTD, mentally recording the license plate number of the other car.

With a silent, primitive scream wedged in the back of her throat, Maggie managed a whispered offer of what she hoped they wanted. "I don't have much money, but—"

"We don't want your money, stupid," the driver snarled.

"Yeah, stupid," repeated the dingbat whose brutal grip was cutting off the circulation in Maggie's arm. "We don't want your money."

That left only one thing, and Maggie's heart sank at the thought. She had always envisioned her first time a bit differently.

"Where are you taking me?" she asked shakily.

"Shut up," the driver ordered.

"Yeah, shut up," the dingbat reiterated.

"Get her down, you idiot, and stop repeating every damned thing I say."

"Get down." The dingbat pushed her to the seat and smashed her face into the plush upholstery. It smelled of cigars and . . . and . . . chili?

Was that a clue?

She'd need to remember all the details for the police report later, she thought optimistically. They would want full descriptions of both men and the car. Right now she refused to think about where they were taking her or what they planned to do when they got there. She would just think about clues.

The men. What could she say? She'd gotten only a glimpse of the guy with echolalia before he'd squashed her down on the seat. He was swarthy and had an unforgivably homely face. He was also outrageously unarmed for a battle of wits. She couldn't see much from her current position, but she could see his shoes. A mugger in wing-tips? They had no unusual marks or decorations—nothing noteworthy there.

The car. Was there anything to identify it other than its peculiar odor? It was dark blue, maybe black. It was medium sized. Not too old, but not new. Maggie didn't know a Ford from a Fiat, so that was no help.

Help?

Nothing could help her now. She should have expected something like this in a big city. Crime was even spreading to her beloved little Sallyville.

Just that afternoon on her way home she'd lost her tote bag to the criminal element. A teenage boy had ripped her off on the bus when she wasn't paying attention. He didn't get much, fortunately. The tote was well worn, her lunch long gone, and she'd been reading her book when he'd robbed her. If theft was his only means of support, Maggie sincerely hoped the young man had better luck with his next victim.

Victim?

Why did she have to think of such a devastating word? Goose bumps rashed out on her arms, and the taste of fear was a metallic bitterness on her tongue. What did they plan to do with her? The ghastly visions conjured up by that question made her ears buzz and apprehensive shivers chase up and down her spine.

Her brain was now running on high-octane terror, and she was overcome by a foreboding that things could only get worse. Maggie whimpered, waiting for her life to pass before her eyes.

What was going down?

Tucker was lucky enough to catch up with them, yet he stayed far enough behind to remain undetected. It could be some of her brothers all the way from Montana, come to fetch her home. Or it could be the organization his department had been trying to tempt out of the woodwork. He didn't know. The only thing he knew for sure was that his suspect had been kidnapped right out from under his nose. That hurt.

Fortunately these were not experienced kidnappers.

She hadn't been chloroformed. Nothing had been thrown over her head to stifle her screams and . . . come to think of it, she hadn't screamed at all. Why not? Maybe they were people she knew. Had the innocent-looking Maggie Ryan double-crossed the double-crossers?

It didn't matter. He had to redeem himself. If Peterson found out about this, Tucker would be back to pounding the pavement and checking out bogus bills passed in supermarkets.

The men in the Caprice weren't exactly being cautious. They didn't bother to take a circuitous route to the abandoned warehouse where they screeched to a halt. Good. Evidently they kept their heads above water only because wood had the ability to float. He didn't need assistance. He could handle this.

Tucker thanked the powers that be for the infirmity of simple minds. If he was able to get the information he needed, he might still come out of all this smelling as sweet as any rose.

Chapter Two

Smelling as sweet as a rose? Make that eau de skunk.

By the time Tucker found another entrance, scaled a wall to get to it and clambered inside, he was huffing and puffing as though he'd just come in last in a marathon. He was getting too old for this, he decided.

He slipped around a mountain of flattened corrugated boxes and worried that the culprits might hear his labored breathing. Not only was he out of breath, but he was also out of bright ideas.

Tucker hadn't anticipated the extra contingent of goons awaiting Maggie's arrival, but by the time he discovered their presence it was too late to call for a backup. Now what? he wondered, and berated himself for not casting his lot with the IRS. Nailing tax evaders in an air-conditioned office beat hell out of his present occupation.

He didn't have time for musing; at the sound of approaching voices Tucker nose-dived beneath the rubble of cardboard. He found himself nose to whisker with a thirty-odd-pound mouser who shot him a go-to-hell look before deciding Tucker was no threat. However, when a rat decided he was and streaked across the floor, Tucker hoped the cat would catch on and follow.

It didn't. Tucker hated cats. Too lazy to try for a moving target, the feline clawed frantically among the boxes in an attempt to flush out a less energetic rodent. The haphazardly stacked cartons swayed threateningly before toppling over in a cardboard avalanche.

Three pairs of oncoming feet clumping through the cavernous warehouse sounded like a herd of stampeding wildebeests to Tucker, and he braced himself for imminent discovery. Peering between the boxes, he could see that the men carried guns and were waving them around the dimly lit area, yelling nervously to each other. "What was that?"

"You think Haversham's got somebody nosing around?"

"How the hell would I know?"

If the finicky cat hadn't chosen that moment to dart out and catch his dinner, Tucker wouldn't have given a plug nickel for his chances. As it was, the men seemed satisfied that the interloper was a four-legged creature and abandoned their search.

At least Tucker had something going for him. Counterfeiters were greedy, which made them careless. They were also usually stupid. That's why they chose the profession for their life's work and why they always got caught. Eventually.

He intended to rescue Maggie, if indeed she required it. But first he wanted to see what information she divulged before he went charging over there. The "how" of his rescue plan hadn't fully crystallized yet, anyway. He would have to play it by ear.

He knew he had compounded his error in judgment by not calling for assistance before entering the warehouse. The department had already succeeded in infiltrating an undercover agent to the other side, but he had no way of knowing who it might be or even if the spy was present among this group. He quietly rearranged the crates to get a better look at the opposition, who were arguing among themselves at the moment. The whole motley crew looked like the local representatives of Thugs-R-Us. But worst of all, the odds were five to one.

Three of them had set up a makeshift spotlight, stationing themselves behind it like interrogators in a bad World War II movie. He imagined they looked pretty menacing to the wild-eyed girl who struggled and squirmed while her captors tried to maintain a tenuous hold on her. They definitely were not her brothers from Montana.

She had grit—he'd give her that. He admired the way Maggie fought them when she had to know she'd have as much chance of getting away as a snowball had in hell. She seemed determined not to make it easy for them, and he was surprised she hadn't fainted or hyperventilated by now. Maybe she wasn't such a mouse, after all.

"Let me go. Take your filthy hands off me," Maggie demanded righteously, feeling like a small dog trying to hide behind its bark.

Stubbornly she pulled, twisting and turning, until she finally managed to clamp her teeth into the arm of one of her captors. He yelped, she yanked an arm free and came up swinging. Maggie knew that tomorrow she would have some unsightly bruises to show for her pitiful efforts, but it was gratifying to know that the kidnapper would have some, too.

Tomorrow? She should live so long.

Quickly and efficiently she was grabbed from behind by a giant. He had to be at least ten feet tall, in Maggie's frightened estimation, and strong enough to go bear hunting with a switch.

"Be still, girlie. I don't want to have to hurt you." The last was whispered gruffly but intimately so that only she would hear—as if they belonged to the same secret club.

Be still? She couldn't even breathe. She couldn't move if her life depended on it. Like a bolt from the blue, the grim reality that it just might streaked across her mind. One beefy arm choked around her neck, cutting off her oxygen, the other squeezed her ribs. Her feet dangled uselessly several inches from the floor. She wasn't going anywhere.

Her frantic mind flashed to a similar set of circumstances involving Clementine Kent. She, too, had been helpless and physically outclassed, but she had managed to outsmart her pursuers by going into the ladies' room and never coming out. Would these guys fall for a trick like that? Maggie glanced from man to man, scrutinizing their faces. It was worth a try.

She decided to pretend compliance until the time came to outmaneuver her assailants.

She felt better for having a plan.

"I can't b-breathe," she gasped dramatically. Her act was complete with fluttering eyelids. "P-please," she begged pitifully. "I-I feel . . . faint."

"Hey, Tiny, you better do something. She won't be no good to us if she can't talk." Maggie couldn't see the man, but if his voice was anything to go by, his disposition was meaner than the famous junkyard dog's. "The boss ain't gonna like it if she croaks before we find out how much she knows."

Tiny dumped her on a crate and none too gently pushed her head between her knees, almost snapping her neck in the process.

Poor little mouse, Tucker sympathized. Please don't faint. Fainting would sabotage any rescue plan he might come up with. Maybe if he jumped out now and held them at gunpoint she would be able to get across the room to his side. That took care of Phase One. Getting the two of them out without any shooting posed a stickier problem. He'd never actually killed anyone and he didn't want to start tonight. Damn. He'd have to wait until she regained her equilibrium and pray for inspiration regarding Phase Two.

Maggie felt sure Tiny's handprint would be forever embedded in the skin on the back of her neck. Surely the police would appreciate the fingerprints.

"I'm okay now," she mumbled around a mouthful of skirt. The pressure eased and she was allowed to raise her head. For the sake of her mental police file, she squinted into the glaring light, trying to get a look at the creeps who were doing this to her. They were all going to pay, she vowed. She was determined.

But she couldn't see a thing. The bright light burned into her eyes, rendering her blind. She lifted her hand for shade. "Who are you? What do you want from me?"

One of the men moved in front of the lamp. He was short and scrawny; his slicked-down hair shone in the lamplight. The term scuzzball came immediately to mind. He smiled at her, a now-I've-got-you-where-I-want-you, weasel-to-a-chicken smile, and a gold tooth caught the light and gleamed menacingly. Maggie half expected him to utter something gangsterish like, "You dirty rat" but instead he grunted, "You ain't bad lookin' for such a big girl."

Maggie's heart stopped and her stomach threatened to disgorge its contents when his sweaty fingers lifted her chin. "You just answer our questions, sweetmeat," he promised in a gritty voice, "and I'll go easy on you when all this is over." The weasel then backed into line with his slimy cohorts.

Tucker felt an unexpected sense of repugnance when the greasy little man touched Maggie, and something inside him almost snapped. He was barely able to hold himself back despite his dislike for the odds against him. That worried him. He was a trained professional with a job to do. Why, then, did he have to keep reminding himself?

Maggie looked pale to him, a little green around the gills. She wouldn't be able to hold out forever.

"Ask her, Tiny. We ain't got all night," the weasely man directed. "You know why she's here."

Tiny turned to Maggie, his face an unreadable mask. "What did you do with it?"

"With what? I don't know what you're talking about."

"The envelope Haversham gave you. What did you do with it?" Tiny's tone brooked no arguments.

"I don't have an envelope. Mr. Haversham never gave one to me. In the month I've been working for him he's never so much as sent me to the post office." Maggie was thoroughly confused by the mention of her boss's name. "Where is Mr. Haversham? He'll tell you he didn't give me any envelope."

Tucker felt like a fool.

All this time he'd thought she was innocent. Man, was that ever a joke. What had she done with the designs? The rescue, if it ever took place, would have to wait until he found out a few more details.

Maggie was so confused. Here she'd been expecting a fate worse than death and they were questioning her about some envelope. Why did they keep insisting she had it when she knew she didn't? "What's in the envelope?" It couldn't hurt to ask.

"I'll ask the questions, girlie," Tiny scolded. "Haversham told us you had it. He told us he gave it to you." The big man bent closer. "Now why don't you tell us where you hid it so we can all go home?"

"Were you by any chance shining a spotlight in Mr. Haversham's face when he gave you this information? I swear to you, I don't have it. I never did. I don't even know what you're talking about." Despite her efforts, twin tears rolled down Maggie's cheeks. She hadn't wanted these men to see her cry. "I answer the phone, do a little dusting. I honestly don't know anything about Mr. Haversham's business or what you're talking about."

What a performance! Tucker would have applauded, but he didn't want to give away his position just yet.

With acid in his voice, Tiny growled, "We went over your apartment with a fine-tooth comb and it ain't there. Who did you pass it to?"

"I told you, I don't have it! I never did." Maggie hiccupped. She always hiccupped when she cried.

Nice touch. Tucker really had to hand it to her—she was good.

Tiny shrugged at the weasel. "We ain't getting nowhere with her. She's too scared to talk, or else she's telling the truth."

"There's only one way to find out," he threatened, his gold tooth flashing in his hateful grin. He moved closer, allowing his fingers to graze her breast as he grabbed her by the shoulders. His intent was about as subtle as a sailor's on a six-hour pass. There was an ominous metallic click and then the flash of a long shiny blade in the lamplight.

My God, Maggie thought with alarm. A knife! Her throat constricted with a scream that wouldn't come out.

"Now, maybe my friend here can help refresh your memory," the weasel intoned.

"Please believe me. I don't know anything." Maggie tried to think about how Clementine would handle the situation, but all thoughts of the spunky detective evaporated in her fear.

The weasel held the knife menacingly near Maggie's face. "I wouldn't want to mess up such a good-looking mug, sister, but don't push me. Cooperate and maybe you and I can have some fun when this is all over," he added lasciviously.

Maggie cringed at what the weasel's idea of "fun" might entail. She hadn't saved herself for this. She had waited to meet the man who could make her want to experience the joy of loving, of giving. She had saved herself for a real and lasting love. Now it looked as if she had saved herself for nothing.

Tucker wondered if they were barking up the right tree.

Did she know more than she was telling? Had Haversham really passed her Skirby's blueprints? Dammit all. He didn't want to believe she was mixed up with the smuggled plans. How could her innocent looks and quiet life-style all be a sham?

Guilty or innocent, Maggie Ryan was his assignment and he had to get her out of there. When he was ready to spring into action, he would have the element of surprise on his side. He would instinctively know when the time was right. Wouldn't he? His thoughts ran like a taximeter at a stoplight—they kept ticking, but they didn't go anywhere.

"Okay, Tiny. Let's see if our little visitor is ready to talk," the weasel hissed.

Maggie felt faint and the room swam around her. Would they ever believe her if she continued to tell the truth? Or could she buy time by feeding them some kind of a lie? She had a good imagination and could probably come up with something, but what would happen to her when the men found out?

No, she decided, almost overcome with fear. She would stick to the truth. They had to believe her. They just had to. She tried to regain control of her galloping emotions and summoned up her t'ai chi training to help calm her shattered nerves. She would put her active imagination to work by pretending that this bad dream was happening to Clementine Kent, who was resourceful, and capable of taking care of herself. She steeled herself and sat up on the crate. This was *not* happening to Maggie Ryan.

Tucker knew she wouldn't be able to hold out very long under the thug's threats. Already her eyes had taken on a vacant, glazed appearance, and he feared she would collapse. He was in pretty good shape, but escaping with an unconscious woman of her stature slung over his shoulder would be difficult at best.

There was no way out of it.

It was time to fish or cut bait, as Pap would say. Time to sneak out alone and go for reinforcements or spring from his hiding place and hope like hell he could get Maggie out in one piece. He sucked in his breath and slid his .38 out of his shoulder holster.

The giant stepped forward and spoke briskly to the guy with the gold tooth. "That's enough. You don't want to scare her so bad that she freezes up, do you?"

The scummy man stepped back and Tucker sighed with relief. They weren't really going to hurt her—they just meant to frighten her enough to get her to talk. All they were after was information. He decided he might learn something yet, so he settled back into his not-so-cozy hideout.

"We're going to take this from the top. Who are you?" The weasel twitched and shifted in agitation. He rubbed his hands together, and Maggie thought he looked at her rather like a hungry dog eyeing a hunk of raw meat.

"Margaret Elizabeth Ryan," she answered slowly, still blinking in the harsh light. She enunciated each word clearly and concisely, so there would be no misunderstanding.

Tiny moved to shield her from the light but the weasel rapidly fired the next question. "Where do you live?"

"Since you just admitted to ransacking my apartment, you should know where I live." Maggie imagined she heard Clementine cheering her on.

The weasel sent her an evil look. "Who do you work for?" He flashed the knife and his metallic grimace, as well.

Maggie frowned; she'd forgotten the question. All she could think about was the weasel's hateful face and the fun he had planned for later. She could do a much better job of concentrating if Tiny asked. He was big and scary looking, but for some inexplicable reason he didn't seem as threatening as the leader of the pack. Maggie giggled. A whole pack of weasels, except for Tiny who was more like a big bear. She must be losing her mind if she could find any humor at all in this. Maybe she was getting hysterical.

Maggie looked at the big man and trembled. "I'm afraid I've forgotten the question," she apologized.

Tiny compressed his lips and a muscle twitched in his jaw. "Who do you work for?"

"Oh. Burl Haversham of Haversham's Photography studio. You know him. The man who ratted on me."

"Don't get cute. Where is the envelope?" Tiny quizzed.

"I don't know."

"Did Haversham give you an envelope?" Tiny wanted to know.

"No." Evidently he didn't like that answer, judging from the scowl on the weasel's face. She was worried that his next step would be to make good on his previous threats.

"We want that damned envelope," the weasel demanded. "What did you do with it?"

He was getting mad at her. "I don't have it." She would have to do better. The man frightened her, and Maggie clutched her purse to her breast. She racked her brain, searching for a way to appease him. What would the cool-headed Clementine have done?

The thug, noticing the protective gesture, grabbed her purse, tore it open and examined the contents. His mean little eyes swiveled back to Maggie. "It's not in here!"

Maggie watched as the weasel dumped everything on the floor, stomping and grinding his heel on each and every item. He looked like Rumpelstiltskin in a snit. "What a mean, spiteful thing to do." Maggie jammed her fists on her hips. She couldn't remember ever seeing such a childish display of temper from an adult.

"Just look what you've done," she yelled. "You've ruined my brand-new lipstick."

"I'm going to ruin a lot more than that if I don't get some answers that I like." With that the little man stubbornly slammed his foot to the floor.

Maggie gasped. "And there go my mints."

"I think she's telling the truth." Tiny turned to his pals. "If she knew anything, she'd have spilled her guts. You scared ten years off her life. I think Haversham pulled a fast one."

"Do you believe me? Can I go now? I've told you everything I know." For the first time, Maggie began to think she might actually survive this night.

The men ignored her questions, choosing to confer among themselves.

She wasn't out of the woods yet.

Tucker didn't trust these hoods. Men like these were dangerous simply because they weren't smart. He would have a hard time second-guessing their next move. If they believed Maggie they just might let her go, but Tucker didn't like the way that slimy jerk was eyeing her. Looked as if he would have to do something after all.

The weasel gave a quick shake of his head and his voice rose in volume when he predicted, "The boss ain't gonna like this."

"The boss, the boss," Tiny mimicked, his tone increasing to thunderous proportions. "You keep talking about the boss. You draw him like a six-gun when you don't know what else to do. If the boss is so smart how did he manage to be double-crossed by a two-bit hood like Haversham? Maybe he ought to come on down here tonight and handle things himself if he thinks you're too stupid to do it right."

There really was no honor among thieves.

Tucker readied himself for anything, as the kidnappers argued among themselves about their next move.

"I've got to go," Maggie interrupted vehemently.

The weasel uttered a savage oath, making her blink. "You ain't going nowhere."

"Okay, then. Something's about to happen that hasn't occurred since I was a toddler." Thank you, Clementine.

"I'll take her to the john." Tiny grasped Maggie's arm and flung his next words over his mountainous shoulder. "You guys decide what we're gonna do with her."

"Be quick about it," the weasel ordered, as if he had already made up his mind what he had in store for Maggie.

This was Tucker's chance.

And he'd thought this would be another yawny, uneventful Friday night in the life of Miss Mousey. All by herself up there in no-man's-land, which was how he had come to think of her apartment. Well, she was surrounded by men tonight, Tucker thought ironically as he wound his way stealthily around the many empty crates and barrels and followed Maggie and her escort to the facilities.

Tiny carefully closed the door behind them. "We don't have much time. You'll have to hurry," he whispered confidentially.

"I'll hurry," Maggie said imperiously as she looked around. "Yuck, this place smells." She turned to Tiny. "You'll have to wait outside the door. I'm modest." She'd already spotted the one window in the room but it was high and narrow. Any red-blooded heroine with a little ingenuity would be able to get out of this predicament.

Tucker hoped Maggie could convince the man to leave her alone for a moment; he was in no hurry to tangle with the big guy.

"Here, take this gun," Tiny instructed. "Hit me, climb out the window and run like the hounds of hell are at your heels."

"Thanks, Tiny." Maggie accepted this new turn of events matter-of-factly. The way things were going this evening, she wouldn't question anything. "I'll go but I don't want your gun."

Was Tiny the department's plant? Tucker wondered.

Overhearing the bizarre exchange, he decided it was entirely possible that Tiny was just a jerk with a soft spot for leggy blondes. If so, he and the man had at least one thing in common.

Tiny slapped the gun firmly in her hand. "Do as I tell you. Hit me, then run."

"I couldn't. I just couldn't." Maggie would not resort to violence and lower herself to her kidnappers' level. She wouldn't be able to live with herself if she did. It went against everything she had ever been taught, all her principles.

You want something done right, you gotta do it yourself.

As quietly as possible, Tucker slipped into the room and drew his arm high over his head. At the last minute he wondered if Tiny and Maggie were in this mess together.

She tossed the gun in the grimy toilet on her mad dash to the window, clambered up onto an overturned wastebasket and hurled herself onto the sill.

She really should thank Tiny for saving her, Maggie thought, and glanced his way just in time to see him crumple to the floor like a felled buffalo. That's when she saw *him*. Her buttoned-down hero from the nightclub. What was he doing here? Was he one of them, too? Could anything else possibly happen to her?

"Dammit woman, haul ass. We ain't got all night!" Tucker pushed her roughly over the ledge and out the window.

Her skirt caught on a nail and stayed behind, billowing like a banner from the corner of the window. Maggie landed with a thud on her bottom and wondered irrationally if she would ever be able to hail a taxi wearing tattered stockings, a black slip and a red sweater.

Just like the real hero she hoped he was, the man sprang like a panther to where she sprawled on the asphalt. All tall, lean and handsome, he bent over her, running his strong hands methodically down her arms.

"You all right?"

"Are you here to rescue me?"

"Sort of," he replied noncommittally, his hands now traveling the length of her legs. "Among other things."

"What are you doing?" she gasped when his hands roamed to her thighs.

Tucker thrust his arms in the air as if she pointed a gun at him. "Nothing. Sorry if my touch is so offensive to you."

"Actually, it was rather nice, but I hardly know you. I mean, I don't *really* know you at all, do I?"

"You don't have any broken bones, but I think it's too early to rule out the possibility of brain damage." What a kook. She might be adorable, but she was still a kook. Smiling ruefully, Tucker pulled Maggie to her feet and propelled her across the road to where he'd hidden his car.

"Hurry," he commanded, shoving her into the car. "We've got to get out of here." He revved the engine and they roared off into the night. And not a minute too soon, judging by the telltale headlights in the rearview mirror. "Looks like we've got company."

Maggie was mesmerized by the dark shadow of evening stubble along his jaw, and her fingertips tingled with a crazy need to discover whether his beard felt hard and bristly or soft and inviting—like his thick brown hair. She was sure she'd never seen a better-looking man, although why she would think of that in her present circumstances was beyond her.

Maggie inched a little closer for further inspection. "You sure are cute." The words were out before she knew they were coming and she decided that her unusually forward behavior, as well as the trembly excitement she felt must be the result of adrenaline aftershock. Or maybe she'd identified with Clementine and her aggressiveness too well.

"Are you sure you didn't land on your head back there?" Tucker frowned at her, wondering if this was the same woman he had nicknamed Miss Mousey. "In the bar tonight you wouldn't so much as dance with a man. You were colder than a miner's behind. But now that our lives are in danger you're hitting on me." Either she was kinky, had rotten timing or was still in shock.

He glanced at her, and the look in her eyes told him she wasn't kidding. He turned his attention back where it belonged.

"I would have danced with you." She smiled invitingly. "But you didn't ask. Why didn't you?"

She had the smokiest green eyes he'd ever seen.

Down, boy, his internal smoke alarm warned—she's a suspect. Maybe she's still confused and frightened or maybe this is all part of her act, so don't go getting any ideas. But Tucker was hard pressed to keep his eyes on the road and his mind on the driving. He almost jumped out of his skin when her hand crept onto his knee. She had asked him a question but he couldn't remember what it was. He was too busy wondering if her actions were her way of trying to get around him, or if she was just a scared kid needing some human contact after her ordeal. "What?"

"Hmm?"

"You asked me something?"

"What's your name?" she asked softly.

"Uh, Tucker." That hand was distracting. "J. P. Tucker." The hand moved slightly, causing an involuntary twitching of a muscle there. He picked up her hand and dropped it into her own lap. "Try that again, later, Legs," he dared. "In a few hours when your adrenaline level is back to normal."

"What does the J.P. stand for? I don't like to use initials."

"Well, I do." They careened onto a residential street on two wheels, and Tucker pressed the pedal to the floor.

Maggie braced herself with her hands and slammed her foot onto an imaginary brake. "Slow down!" she yelled. "Are you trying to kill us?"

A bullet shattered the back window before Tucker could answer. "No. I'm just trying to keep those guys from doing the job." He waved frantically at the car chasing them around another hair-raising turn. They sped through an alley, sideswiping garbage cans and sending debris flying into the air and onto the car.

They were using real bullets, Maggie realized. This was no fantasy. "Why are those men shooting at us? Who are you, anyway? What have you done?" she screamed unreasonably.

Drastic actions were sometimes called for.

Tucker grabbed a handful of blond curls and squashed Maggie's face into the seat. "Stay down, dammit!"

The tears she'd felt coming on all evening now overflowed onto the no-frills upholstery of Tucker's car. This was the second time tonight someone had pressed her face into a car seat and she was getting damned tired of it. What had she ever done in her life to deserve this kind of treatment?

She always tried to be kind and helpful; she was basically a decent, tax-paying, law-abiding citizen. She helped out with the Special Olympics, bought charity tickets from the fire department, the police and the Art League. She had a standing cookie order with the Girl Scouts. All her life she had been loved and protected by her family. She did not deserve this abuse.

Why had she gone to that damned club with Holly? Being a good sport had gotten her into one hell of a predicament tonight. She had been robbed on the bus, kidnapped, held at gunpoint, groped by a weasel and threatened with a knife. And now she was being shot at! She was being used as target practice by God-only-knew-who, while being driven in the opposite direction from home by a lunatic with a death wish.

They made one maniacal turn after another to the tune of bullets pinging against the car. "What are you trying to do?" she yelled.

"I'm trying to lose them."

"Is it working?" she asked from her position below the dashboard.

"No."

Great. This was crazy. What was even crazier, Maggie realized, was that the frustrated stunt driver was the first man she'd ever felt physically attracted to. He was the first man to make her heart stutter, her pulses throb, her senses swim, her knees weaken. But then again, she had to admit, her reaction might just as well be a sensible fear for her life.

She stole a covert glance at his strong profile, silhouetted by the street lamps as they streaked by. No, it was him. But for all she knew about him he could be Arlington's answer to Jack the Ripper.

Her despair reached new heights and she bawled at the injustice of it all.

For crying out loud! Tucker thought. That was the most woebegone sound he'd ever heard. He'd like to hold her in his arms and...do what? Anything it took to make that sound stop. If he hadn't had his hands full he would have done just that.

Hang on, Legs. I'll get you out of this if it's the last thing I do, he vowed silently. He also hoped fervently that it would not be.

Chapter Three

It was deathly quiet.

The gunfire had suddenly ceased, along with Maggie's tears. Clementine Kent had never been killed or even seriously maimed in any of the high-speed chases Maggie had read about. She kept her wits about her when the going got tough. She wouldn't be caught dead blubbering like a baby or lying helplessly in the front seat. She would be urging her man to drive faster. And she'd be shooting back.

But Maggie couldn't shoot back; she'd left Tiny's gun sinking in the toilet back at the warehouse. She would have liked to sit up, but Tucker still had an iron grip on her hair.

"Uh, Tucker?" she ventured.

"Yeah?" He was relieved she'd finished. All that bawling made him want to hold her in his arms, made him want to caress away the hurt. It was the tears that made him want to do all those things, he told himself. And that's all it was.

"Do you think you could let go of my hair now?" she snapped. "It hurts."

"Oh, sorry." He glanced down at his hand, surprised to find it still clasped around the silky softness of her palomino curls. He forced his fingers to relax, loosening his grip, but he was loath to remove his hand entirely.

"Uh, Tucker?"

"What?"

"Can I sit up now?" The wild turns seemed behind them, but they were practically flying and Maggie felt the only way they could go any faster would be for the car to suddenly sprout wings.

With great effort Tucker pulled his hand away from her. "I suppose so. We seem to have lost them. For a while, anyway."

"That's wonderful." She wound her arms around his neck in a grateful, exuberant hug. "You're wonderful. We're safe." She was glad to be alive and wanted to share her joy with him.

Tucker enjoyed the spontaneous gesture until he opened his eyes and saw the rapidly approaching headlights of an oncoming car. He flung Maggie against the back of the seat with his right arm and with his left managed to swerve out of its path just in time.

"I'm sorry if my touch is so offensive, Tucker."

He pinched the bridge of his nose with his thumb and forefinger. "That's just the problem," he muttered.

"There's no need to get rough," she said. "If you don't like it, all you have to do is say so."

He fought valiantly but finally gave in to the compelling urge to smile. "I should have said," he explained, "I don't find it offensive at all. Actually I enjoyed it. *That's* the problem." Problem? That was an understatement. He wiped the grin from his face—this was business. He had a job to do. Now was no time to give in to his baser instincts. They might still be in danger. As soon as they got to D.C. she would be Peterson's problem—sultry voice, temporary insanity, legs and all. Whether she was guilty or not, it didn't really matter. The department would put her in protective custody and he would be reassigned. And that, he told himself smugly, would be that.

Maggie stared at the determined look that washed over Tucker's face and wondered if the paralyzing fear she'd known earlier had altered her ability to think rationally. Her senses tingled and her awareness of what was going on around her was heightened. Boy, was she aware. But how could she be so attracted to a complete stranger? So unconcerned about his role in all that had transpired? Where had he come from? Why was he here? And why on earth wasn't she finding out?

"Tucker?"

"Hmm?" This time he kept his eyes glued to the road, refusing to look at her. Every time he did, something crazy happened.

"Are you one of the bad guys or what?" Would he admit it if he was?

Tucker snorted. "If so, you'd be in one hell of a mess, wouldn't you?" She was thinking, and that was a good sign—no permanent brain damage from her fall from the window. "No, Maggie. I'm not one of them."

"Whew, I'm glad to hear that." Just like that, she believed him. But she couldn't help wondering if she truly thought him trustworthy or if she just wished him to be.

They passed under another series of street lamps and Maggie noticed her ravaged panty hose. "Criminy. How tacky."

"What's tacky?"

"These stockings are ruined. I can't wear these."

"What are you doing?" he barked as he ran over the curb. Did she realize how provocative she looked? Her slim hips wriggled on the seat; then she raised one leg and began sliding the nylons down its shapely length.

"Taking them off."

And throwing them out the window.

In his best G-man voice Tucker cautioned, "Littering is against the law, Maggie."

"So is running a stop sign," she pointed out casually.

He slammed on his brakes but he was already through the intersection. Damn! He wasn't sure he could function under such duress. Nothing in his years of experience had prepared him for driving at high speed with a half-dressed woman in the front seat.

Especially a woman like this one. It was definitely time to pass the torch and get her off his hands and into Peterson's.

He pulled into a busy all-night service station and parked by a telephone booth. "I've got to make a call. You stay put," he ordered, opening his door.

Maggie yanked her own door open. "I think I'll take advantage of this pit stop if you don't mind."

"Do you think that's wise?" he drawled, his eyes gliding sensuously over her dainty, frilly slip, which struck her at midthigh. His gaze roamed lazily all the way down to the no-nonsense black pumps on her slender feet.

Maggie's eyes followed the path he set. "Oh," she gasped, and slammed her door. Not only was she with a devastating stranger, but she was in her underwear. This was not turning out to be one of her better nights.

She watched Tucker's tall, well-built form as he strode into the phone booth, closed the door and leaned against it. His stance emphasized the force of his thighs and the slimness of his hips. The bright light of the booth gave her a clear view, and she admired the inherent strength of his ruggedly handsome face, the firm yet sensual line of his lips and the set of his chin, which suggested a stubborn streak. It would not be difficult to wake up in the mornings and get lost in his long-lashed chocolate-colored eyes. Lord. What kind of thoughts were those to be having at a time like this?

Unable to force her gaze from him, she flinched when he slammed the phone into its cradle and banged his fist on the fat phone book. She wondered whom he had called and what had made him so angry.

Scowling, Tucker closed the car door with a thud and started the engine before he spoke. "Looks like we're stuck with each other for a while," he grumbled.

"Stuck?" she repeated incredulously. "All you have to do is take me home. So you really aren't *stuck* with me at all." It hurt that he didn't enjoy her company as much as she was enjoying his.

"I can't take you home," he snapped. His eyes flashed angrily.

"Well, I can't exactly take public transport dressed like this. Just how do you expect me to get there?" How much was one person expected to take? "In the past eight hours I've been robbed, kidnapped, groped, held at knife point and shot at. Then you come along, rip the clothes right off my body and drive me through the streets of Arlington like you've never seen those ads that warn, 'Don't try this in your own car.' This has not exactly been a fun-filled evening for me!"

She was screaming. She never screamed. Yet here she was yelling like a demented banshee at a perfect stranger.

Tucker made it a policy to always give as good as he got. "Well, it hasn't been the highlight of my life, either!" He peeled out of the parking lot and sped off down the street into the bleakest night he could ever remember.

Maggie sniffed and Tucker feared the waterworks would start again. "Those men know where you live. Do you honestly think you can just nonchalantly go home?"

She sniffed again, knowing he was right and hating him for it. Unreasonably, she accused, "It's your fault my skirt is hanging from a windowsill somewhere."

"My fault?" he retorted, his tone disbelieving. "My fault? We'd have been dead meat if we'd spent another ten seconds in that damned warehouse. I only pushed you because I thought you were coming back inside."

"I wanted to see if Tiny was all right," she mumbled in self-defense. "You didn't kill him, did you?"

"Now that takes the prize," he said sarcastically.

"Did you?" She could be stubborn herself when the situation merited it.

"No. I rang his bell. Hell, he was probably in that car chasing us. It could have been your old buddy Tiny who was shooting at us back there! And you're worried about him?"

"Oh. I didn't think about that."

Maggie wedged herself against the dash as Tucker wheeled into a parking garage without slowing down. He applied the brakes at the last possible moment and did not come to a full stop until the nose of the car rested against the automatic arm blocking the entrance.

He inserted a funny-looking plastic card in the meter and the arm rose. Tucker laid rubber, taking off with a burst of speed that would only have been warranted had someone fired a starting pistol.

Maggie clenched her jaw. "Slow down, dammit."

Tucker ignored her and continued his one-car competition. On the third level he veered into an empty space and braked to a sudden stop at a concrete wall. Now Maggie could add whiplash to her ever-growing list of the evening's indignities. She would have liked to go home and soak in a hot tub of bubbles. Maybe lose herself in a good novel. But no more mysteries, no more intrigue or adventure. She'd miss Clementine, but she'd had all she wanted for a while.

When her door jerked open, Maggie whipped around in surprise. "What?"

"Get out," he ordered.

"Why?" No self-respecting heroine allowed a hero to talk to her like that and get away with it.

"We have to get a different car. One they won't be looking for." He forgot to be angry when her slip slid up her legs as she turned to get out of the car. His eyes followed the sensuous trail of the silken material up her slender thighs and his hands literally ached to follow the same path.

"Oh," she said absently, watching him watch her. All her previous thoughts about going home, and her anger at Tucker, dissolved like sugar in the rain. Pure and simple magic. That's what it was.

"Let's go," he commanded. What was it about her that turned his brain to oatmeal? You'd think he'd never seen bare legs before. Disgusted with himself and his physical response to the woman, Tucker propelled her across the empty garage to the elevator and hauled her inside.

"I love it when you get all forceful," she said with a malicious little smile.

"We don't have all night, you know."

"So you keep telling me."

As the doors slid shut he punched every floor button from four to ten. If anyone was tailing them, watching from below, they would not know when they left the elevator.

During the brief elevator ride something deep and compelling made Tucker aware of her as a woman, not as a suspect or an assignment. When he turned to her his gaze was as soft as a caress. His eyes dropped involuntarily from hers, roaming to her neck, her shoulders, her breasts.

Maggie felt mesmerized. But an intensity flared through her entrancement, and she suffered a formidable need to be close to his long, lean body.

The elevator opened and Tucker's hand snaked into his leather jacket, seeking the comforting weight of his revolver. No one got on or off. When the same thing happened the second time Maggie felt a little like Alice. Things were getting curiouser and curiouser.

"I thought we were getting a car."

Tucker ignored her.

"Do you own the car in question? Have you forgotten where it's parked?"

He took a deep breath, refusing to answer, and merely looked straight ahead.

"Or are we just shopping around until we find something we want to steal?" she gibed.

"I'm following orders," he snapped. Had he really compared this woman to a mouse? A mouse? Hah! Every time he looked at her something tingled somewhere. No mere mouse of a woman had ever had that effect on him before.

"Whose orders?"

"My superior's."

"Would that, by any wild stretch of the imagination, be the same superior the weasel and Tiny were arguing about tonight?"

The weasel? Yeah, he could buy that. "I'm a Secret Service agent, employed by the Treasury Department." He reached into his breast pocket and flashed his badge at her.

The elevator stopped on the eighth floor and Tucker tried to take her arm, but she jerked away. "That looked official. But I don't know what all this has to do with me," she said, trotting to keep up with his long stride.

They stopped behind a blue sedan with blackwall tires, and Tucker ran his fingers under the rear bumper until he found the metal box that held the key. "You're a suspect," he clipped, thinking he would do well to remember that.

"A suspect?" Maggie gasped for breath to add to the force of her next question. "Suspected of what?"

"We'll talk about this later. When you're a bit more coherent." He helped her into the car. "You've had a pretty bad scare tonight, and fear can jumble a person's reasoning."

He was telling *her*. And now she was a suspect. Suspect? She was a victim. He'd better believe they would discuss this later, and she wanted details.

When he was satisfied they weren't being followed and had left the city lights far behind them, Tucker gestured at the back seat.

When he'd checked in on the phone and received the bad news that he would be Maggie's temporary guardian, Tucker had insisted that a less revealing set of clothing be provided for her. "There's supposed to be some clothes for you in here somewhere. Why don't you see if you can find them?" He kept his eyes on the highway, refusing to look at her. He couldn't afford to make that mistake again.

Maggie crawled into the back seat, found a brown paper bag and dumped its contents in her lap. "I think these clothes are used." They were definitely secondhand, she thought, as she sifted through them. There was a well-worn pair of jeans, a faded T-shirt with a slogan across the front that she couldn't quite make out in the darkness, and a disreputable-looking pair of sneakers of indiscernible color.

Tucker stifled a grin. "I imagine all the better stores were closed at this hour. Why don't you slip into something a little less comfortable?" And a lot less revealing.

"Here?"

"Sure. Why not?"

Maggie could think of several reasons, like a reluctance to wear clothing that was probably pinched from some agent's gym locker and dressing without complete privacy. Growing up as the baby sister of four brothers had assured her of never wearing hand-me-downs, and the entire family had respected her innate shyness. After what she had been through so far, Maggie wasn't sure she was up to putting on a show for J. P. Tucker.

"When you're dressed you can come back up here and help me watch for a place to stay tonight."

She glanced at him in alarm. They were going to spend the night somewhere? Well, she reasoned, it was late and they had to sleep, so why not? The idea actually seemed logical in the face of the bizarre events of the evening. Wrinkling her nose at the secondhand clothing, Maggie decided to humor him. She'd feel a lot less vulnerable once she was fully dressed.

Maggie kicked off her shoes and dropped them into the grocery bag. Leaving her slip on, she tugged the slim-fitting jeans upward and struggled diligently with the metal buttons until each was securely fastened.

Try as he might, Tucker couldn't keep his roving eyes from the rearview mirror, and he watched her lightning-quick movements in fascination. He shook his head when she yanked on the sneakers without bothering to tie the laces. He almost laughed out loud when he heard the slight ripping sound and the whispered "Damn" as she shimmied out of the skimpy slip. Her breathing was rapid from her exertions when she spoke.

"Why did you slow down?" She paused for a quick breath. "Are we stopping?"

Tucker tore his eyes from the mirror and speeded up a bit. "As soon as I find a place. I don't know about you," he lied, "but I'm bushed." What was the matter with him? he chastised himself. Why was he watching that mirror like a schoolboy who had discovered a peephole to the girls' locker room? Unlike the schoolboy, he couldn't see a thing.

Maggie couldn't remember being quite so tired. "Me too," she mumbled as she tried to figure out a way to get into the T-shirt without first removing her sweater.

When his wayward glance sought the mirror again, Tucker thought she was going to wear the shirt over the sweater. Instead she removed her arms from the sweater sleeves, and he watched enthralled as the T-shirt disappeared inside the shapeless garment. She was ingenious. She'd changed tops without showing more than two inches of bare skin at her midriff.

Tucker had been so engrossed in Maggie's antics in the back seat that he almost missed the small motel's winking neon sign. But with a bit of artful maneuvering he managed to exit at the correct turnoff.

"Looks like the coffee shop is still open. We'll go in and get something to go," Tucker told Maggie as he parked.

Maggie wasn't hungry, but she was too tired to argue. Besides, it appeared that J. P. Tucker, agent extraordinaire, was in charge. She was just along for the ride.

Once in the room, Maggie stowed the grocery bag containing her meager belongings in the closet and plopped facedown on the mock-brass double bed. With a "what-now" sigh, she watched Tucker check out the place, grudgingly admitting to herself that she felt safer in his company than she had since leaving Montana.

He made sure the door was secure from the inside as well as from the outside, then pocketed the key. "I'm going to wash up. You stay put," he commanded before disappearing into the tiny bathroom.

"Yes, master," Maggie grumbled under her breath. Not even her four older brothers had been so damned bossy, and she was quickly learning to resent Tucker's high-handed manner. She also resented the way he kept her in the dark about everything that had happened.

What had happened, anyway? she wondered. Why was she in a strange motel with an even stranger man? Some pretty outlandish things had taken place tonight, and it was a wonder she wasn't totally hysterical. Maggie glanced down at the shirt she wore and gasped. That she was wearing a T-shirt urging Let's Get Physical was the most outlandish thing of all.

The key word was *envelope*, an envelope her boss had allegedly confessed to giving her. What had those maniacs done to poor Mr. Haversham to make him say such a thing—if he really had? She had a good mind to call him and see if he knew what was going on.

That's exactly what she should do. Maggie twisted around to reach for the phone. On the seventh ring, she decided that Mr. Haversham was either out or not answering. She recalled the weasel's knife with a shudder and wouldn't let herself think of any other reason why he might fail to answer. A knot of panic formed in her stomach, and she replaced the phone just as Tucker stepped back into the room.

"Who was on the phone?" he asked sharply.

"Nobody."

"Don't give me that. I saw you hang up. Who did you call?" If she wanted to play games he'd go along for a while, but he was quickly running out of patience.

Maggie sat up on the edge of the bed and glared back at him. "I tried to call Mr. Haversham to find out if he knows anything about all of this—since you're so tight-lipped."

"Is that a fact?"

"Yes, it is. I'm not used to this kind of craziness. Believe it or not, Tucker, most of the time I live a relatively quiet life."

"That's what you'd like me to believe," he countered as he retrieved the fragrant bag of burgers he'd purchased at the coffee shop.

"It's the truth, but I don't really care if you believe me or not, now that I think of it. You'll just have to trust me." Maggie caught the foil-wrapped sandwich he tossed her.

"In my business, you don't trust anyone." He unwrapped his burger and began to eat hungrily. It frustrated him that he hadn't been able to peg Maggie Ryan. Half the time he thought she was Rebecca of Sunnybrook Farm, and the other half he was sure she was mixed up with Haversham and Skirby. But as he watched her examine her burger desultorily, a little-girl-lost look on her face, he wavered. Who was she really?

"What's the matter? Aren't you hungry?" he asked.

"I'm sorry, but having my life threatened usually dulls my appetite. However, it hasn't affected yours, I see."

Tucker picked up an onion ring and closed his teeth over half the crisply fried vegetable. "Nope. I live for excitement," he teased. When their gazes locked, Maggie ran her tongue over her lips and his heart missed a beat. "Want some?" he offered softly.

"Some what?" she stalled, her eyes still on his mouth. She'd forgotten exactly what she did want, but she was reasonably sure it had nothing to do with food. Every time he looked at her, her heart turned over in response. She wished he were a troll, with the skin and bulging eyes of a toad, so she could summon up enough resistance to kick him out of her room. Or at the very least, why couldn't she have drawn a balding, middle-aged family man three months from retirement as her custodian?

Tucker's insides jangled with anticipation as he moved closer, all the while fighting the reasons why he shouldn't. But, he acknowledged grimly, his feelings for her had nothing to do with reason.

"Ah, Maggie," he murmured with a gentle smile that turned her bones to water.

His invitation was a passionate challenge, impossible to resist, too powerful to deny. He swept her, weightless, into his arms and claimed her lips for his own. His mouth was warm and moist, his kiss flipped the pit of Maggie's stomach into a swirl and made her ache for more.

She kissed him back with a hunger he hadn't expected, an intensity he'd never felt in a woman before. Her lips were more persuasive than he cared to admit, and he felt the shock waves roll through his body. It was the kind of kiss a man would want if he could only have one in his lifetime.

Leaving her mouth burning with his fire, Tucker's lips blazed a trail to the pulsing hollow at the base of her throat. Her eager response to the slow, drugging kisses shocked her, but Maggie could not find rationality among her whirling senses. He left her throat and seared a path to her shoulder, up her neck, gently biting her earlobes before finally smothering her lips with demanding mastery. His tongue traced, explored and devoured the fullness of her lips and sent shivers of desire racing through her.

As Tucker roused her passion, his own grew stronger. The blood pounded in his brain and made him tremble with need, need for Maggie. His palm slid lovingly, possessively over one sensitive breast. He felt her warm flesh surge at his touch and reason tried to reassert itself. He couldn't remember laying her down or curling her body to his. How had it happened? When had he lost all control?

Reluctant but determined, Tucker throttled the dizzying currents skidding through him and tore his lips from hers. But he couldn't tear his gaze from her eyes, which had turned a smoldering mix of green and brown.

His hoarse whisper broke the silence. "I'm sorry, Maggie. I shouldn't have done that." He felt like the lowest form of life, taking advantage of her when he knew she was probably traumatized with fright and her defenses were down. Aside from that, he had absolutely no business making love with a suspect. Some protective custodian he had turned out to be!

"I'm not. I'm glad you kissed me," she murmured in a low, husky tone. These sensations were so new to her, and so overwhelming, that she felt compelled to be honest. "I've never experienced anything quite like it. It was probably the single most beautiful thing that ever happened to me." But hearing her thoughts on her own lips embarrassed her. He didn't want her, and she had never wanted anyone more.

He cupped her chin, raising her pain-filled eyes level with his own remorseful ones. "I didn't mean it that way, Maggie."

"It's okay, Tucker. You don't have to explain anything. I understand. If you don't like it, you don't like it." Rejection happened to everyone at one time or another.

"I liked it, Maggie." He let out a long audible breath. "I more than liked it. But I'm sort of on duty. I mean, you're in protective custody. *My* protective custody." He felt like a fool confessing such a thing while his hand rested on her breast. He rolled to his back to distance himself from her magnetic charms. He needed a lot of distance. Like a few light-years. Throwing one last, long regretful look at her on the rumpled bed, he put his hands to his head. Slowly he began to laugh.

Maggie stared at him in disbelief. She knew she was inexperienced and guileless where men were concerned, but surely she was not an object of humor. "What?"

"Oh, Maggie, just look at this bed. It's filled with bits of hamburger, onion rings and catsup. The maid is going to have some juicy gossip on her break tomorrow."

She surveyed the mess with amused wonder, her gentle laugh rippling in the air. When she finally got to her feet she said, "You made the mess; you tidy it up before you let yourself out. I'm going to take a bath and go to bed." She didn't wait for an answer before she went into the bathroom and closed the door.

A second later she reopened it and poked her head around the corner. "Good night, Tucker."

Tucker's smile blossomed. "Good night, Maggie."

Chapter Four

What a great pair of legs.

Tucker thoroughly enjoyed the scenery of Maggie's long slim limbs as she backed out of the bathroom wearing nothing but the baggy, thigh-length sweater. He already knew there was nothing wrong with the rest of her; she was hiding no unsightly flaws after all. "I never thought I'd be saying this, but I love that sweater."

Maggie whirled around in surprise, dropping the wet clothes to the floor. "I thought you were supposed to tidy up and let yourself out?" But here he was—as big as life and twice as sexy. And he was in her bed! From the looks of him, he wore little more than the sheet across his lean hips, or was that wishful thinking on her part?

"I cleaned up the mess." He gestured to the corner where he'd stuffed the bedspread and the debris of their late dinner. "What happened? Did you forget to take your clothes off before you stepped into the tub?"

He knew quite well what had happened to her clothes—he was planning to rinse the food stains out of his own as soon as she was finished in the bathroom. Something perverse in him just liked to watch her blush.

Maggie retrieved the clothes and scurried to the closet for hangers. She couldn't let him witness the flush that was already beginning to make her ears burn. Merely thinking about how the mustard and catsup stains had come to be all over her jeans, shirt and even her bra initiated an infuriating wave of crimson. She snatched her torn half-slip from the brown bag that served her as luggage and shimmied into it. She shot him a malevolent look as she hung her wet things to dry and tried to think of a clever retort.

"Come on, Maggie," he teased. "I'm dying to hear. How did your clothes get wet?"

"Don't change the subject. Why are you still here?" Gingerly she sat down on the edge of the bed, not sure what she wanted his answer to be. He lay there, devilishly handsome and appealing, a lazy, seductive look on his face.

He lowered his gaze and his voice and tried to hide the longing he felt. A longing to gather her into his arms. "I wish I were in another room. Right now, I'd prefer to be on another planet. But I have a job to do."

"And I'm it?" She drew an invisible pattern on the crisp white sheet. She didn't want to hear that; she wanted him to tell her he was mad about her, he couldn't live without her and that he craved her. That's what always happened to Clementine Kent. It was only fair—a reward for enduring all she had to endure.

Maggie didn't understand why she felt the way she did. Maybe it was because she and Tucker had been through more together tonight than many couples experience in a lifetime. Maybe struggling for survival had a way of cutting through all the superficial proprieties—the same phenomenon that prompted so many wartime marriages. Whatever it was that she was feeling, it hurt to know he didn't feel the same.

"I'm afraid so. My orders are not to let you out of my sight and to use the handcuffs if necessary. I've already disobeyed the first command, but I guess I can't haul you into the bathroom with me. All you have to do is promise you won't try to get away and I won't use the cuffs."

Maggie clamped her fists together, thrusting them at him. "How can you trust a suspect? Cuff me!" she said, her voice frigid.

"You're not my prisoner, Maggie, you're in protective custody. So just give me your word."

"If you think I'm going to stay in this room with you tonight simply because you've been ordered, you're wrong." She'd be damned if she would willingly let a man sleep in her bed *in the line of duty.*

"Where can you go dressed like that? Your clothes are still wet," he pointed out reasonably.

"I don't care. I refuse to stay with you under these circumstances." If she were handcuffed, it would no longer be her choice and she wouldn't have to feel guilty about spending the night in a motel with a strange man.

"Okay, you asked for it, you stubborn little thing." Tucker flung back the sheet and jumped out of bed in a huff but little else.

Maggie's eyes widened appreciatively, taking in his tempting, attractive male physique. His powerful chest was broad and muscular and covered with just the right amount of crisp brown hair. Hair that fanned over well-developed pectorals and stemmed down to his . . . Her eyes froze momentarily on the white boxer shorts he wore. They were covered with big red hearts. Her gaze met his and they locked for a moment in mutual amusement. She lost it first, but soon his deep-timbred laugh joined in.

"I don't want to use these," he said, waving the manacles he'd retrieved from his jacket.

Maggie sobered instantly at sight of the ugly metal handcuffs. "I won't stay here if you don't. I'll say good-night now, and don't think it hasn't been lovely, Tucker."

"Dammit." He strode to her side of the bed, clamped one of the cuffs to the imitation brass headboard and locked her right wrist in the other. "When you're ready to cut the crap, I'll take them off."

With that he stalked around to his own side, plopped onto the bed and closed his eyes. "Good night," he said tersely.

"Oh, Tucker?" she sang sweetly.

He sat up expectantly and flashed her his ever-ready smile. "Yes?"

"You forgot to turn off the light."

He muttered a pithy oath, glared at her, then torpedoed out of bed and slapped off the overhead light by the door. On the way back he let go with another choice epithet as he stubbed his toe on the footboard.

"Did you hurt yourself?" she asked with fake concern when he yanked the covers.

"No."

"Too bad."

Tucker rolled as far as possible to his side of the bed, clinging to the edge of the mattress with a death grip. Finally he felt her tug at the sheet, settling in. Man, it was going to be the longest night of his life.

Why did she have to be so pigheaded?

Time passed slowly. From her movements, Tucker knew she was having difficulty drifting off. He ought to take those damned cuffs off, wrap her in his arms and go to sleep. After all, if she moved so much as a muscle, he'd wake up. Wake up? What a joke. If he wrapped her in his arms he wouldn't waste time sleeping. And if she moved so much as a muscle, he'd...

Don't torture yourself, Tucker, he cautioned. You're already about to explode.

"Tucker," Maggie whispered in the darkness.

This was it. She was ready to give in. But he'd let her suffer a little longer by feigning sleep. Although her movements were subtle, he knew she must really be uncomfortable.

"Tucker?" she ventured again.

"Yes?"

"Where did you get the cutesy undies?"

He hadn't seen that one coming. "They were given to me." He hoped to avoid a lengthy explanation of how he had come to own such an outrageous garment as well as why he was wearing it now.

His answer only filled her mind with more questions. She hadn't even stopped to consider his marital status. Surely no man would wear anything like that unless his wife was there to see that he did. "From your wife?" She held her breath.

"I'm not married."

When she breathed again it was with satisfaction. "Then who gave them to you?"

"Will you stop flouncing around and go to sleep!" As a young boy Tucker had often chanted incantations to change things he had no control over. He mentally composed one now. Abracadabra, don't make a peep. Shut your eyes and fall asleep. Good try but he noted that it still didn't work.

"I know. Your mother." Maggie smiled in the inky room.

"I don't have a mother."

"Sorry. A girlfriend, then?"

"I don't have girlfriends, either."

"Oh?" She drew out the word in a definite question.

Tucker turned on the bedside light. "I should have phrased that differently. I don't have *steady* girlfriends." He massaged his forehead with the heels of his hands. "Do you want to watch TV or something?"

"Or something," she decided.

A brow arched and he regarded her carefully. "Which means?"

"I'd like to talk. I just wanted to know what happened to her."

"Her? Her who?" Had he missed something?

"The girlfriend who gave you the heart-o'-my-heart shorts."

Tucker shook his head in an attempt to clear the cobwebs. He *had* missed something.

"Well, she must have been very special," Maggie persisted.

"Oh, yes, my mythical girlfriend again. She wasn't."

"But she must have been. I mean, if you're willing to parade around in those dumb-looking shorts and all."

Tucker shrugged. "She was just a one-night fling."

"Is it protocol for a 'fling' to give you a valentine like that?"

"Protocol?"

"I'm not too well versed in mating manners, and I wondered if it's standard procedure for the woman to give a gift to the pickup of her choice? Or is that custom reserved for holidays?"

There was no way out—he'd have to tell her. "I was in a nightclub, drinking. I met a woman, we danced, I took her home and we had a good time together. Later, when I was dressing, I couldn't find my briefs so she rummaged around and gave me these. That's it. It happened a long time ago. Satisfied?"

"She must have made some kind of impression."

He sighed. "Not really. Why?"

"You still wear them."

He was getting tired of this conversation. "I ran out of clean laundry. Okay? If they bother you so much, I guess I could get rid of them..."

His sudden movement toward nudity alarmed Maggie. "No. That won't be necessary."

"What a relief. Now could we just dispense with those handcuffs and get some sleep?"

"No."

Tucker glared at her, shrugged, then clicked off the light. His head had barely touched the pillow when her restless movements began again. Quickly he switched on the lamp. "What *are* you doing?"

"T'ai chi ch'uan." One arm wound slowly over her head. "It works better using both arms, but I'll manage."

Tucker bit back a smile. "It looks very strange."

"I'm getting rid of my stress."

"Do you have to do it now?" he grumbled, thinking he hadn't had any stress until he'd met her.

"I can't sleep. I'm too wound up. I have to do this." She dropped her arm to her side and eyed him hopefully. "Unless you'd like to talk a while. Talking always helps me relax."

Choosing the lesser of two evils, Tucker built himself a backrest with pillows and settled back, folding his arms over his chest. "Okay. You win. We'll talk."

Maggie made herself as comfortable as the handcuffs would permit. "What do you do to relieve tension and stress? Run? Work out? What?" She was sure he did something in a gym—one did not acquire muscles like his through genes alone.

"I whittle."

"What kind of things do you whittle?"

"You don't whittle *things*. You just take big sticks and make them smaller."

"Wonderful. Who taught you—your father?"

"My grandfather. Pap always said busy hands were happy hands, and he kept me pretty occupied. And I guess it's true because I was never happier than when I was with Pap."

Maggie noticed the fond glimmer that rose in Tucker's eyes when he spoke of his grandfather. She could tell he loved him very much.

"I always wanted to be just like him. I used to sit for hours mimicking the way he slouched against the porch rail, the way he'd spit tobacco juice over the tip of his boots out into the yard." He chuckled, and Maggie watched his eyes soften even more as he added, "I'd chew on wild mint until I'd get a good-sized wad in my mouth. Sometimes, I'd let a dribble leak out of the corner just so I could wipe it on my shirtsleeve like he did."

"Tell me about Pap. He sounds delightful." Both sets of Maggie's grandparents had passed away before she'd been old enough to remember anything about them. She'd always missed that in her life.

Tucker considered. With any luck he might just be able to talk her to sleep. That seemed to be the only way either of them would get any rest tonight. "Pap is quite a character. I'm always spouting things he used to say to me, like those comparisons that make country speech so colorful."

"Like what?" she prompted.

"Like 'hotter'n a beanfield in hell.' 'Darker'n the inside of a snuff can.'" Tucker observed Maggie's rapt expression. "'Cuter'n a speckled pup.' That sort of thing. I've never talked about him much. What do you want to know?"

"Did he live with your family?"

"Pap *was* my family. It was always just me and Pap. I never knew my father, since my mother was unmarried. That makes me illegitimate."

"You're a love child," Maggie mused. "I've always heard they're special. Exceptionally bright. Sensitive."

"Don't kid yourself." Tucker grinned. "Do you always look for a rose among the thorns?"

"Sure. Doesn't everybody?" Maggie smiled and Tucker noticed her dimples for the first time. Two of them. "What did Pap think about your situation, Tucker?"

"He never gave any opinion that I can recall. But I once asked him about my father and he said, 'Sprout, I don't know your pa, but he must have been quite a man because you are one fine boy.' He was good to me. And he taught me a lot."

Maggie's heart swelled at the thought of what Tucker might have missed in life. "Was he affectionate?" She couldn't imagine growing up without the love of her big, caring family.

"Well, Pap never got all mushy the way mothers probably do, but I knew he loved me. He tickled me, ruffled my hair... things like that. He was always there for me."

"How old were you when you lost your mother?"

"I didn't lose her; she lost me. She moved to Norfolk after I was born, leaving me with Pap until she could get on her feet. I guess it took a long time. Too long. Because when she finally decided she wanted me back, I didn't want to go. I wanted to stay with Pap, and that seemed to suit him, too.

"We exchanged a few letters. She visited at Christmas, birthdays and such. But as I got older we grew further apart."

"You've lost contact with her?" Maggie thought of her own warm, boisterous family and was filled with sadness.

"Pap mentions her in his letters or when I go to visit him. He manages to tell me what she's doing, how her life is going."

"What does she do?"

"She got married a few years ago to a widower with two teenage daughters and finally retired to become a full-time wife and mother. They live on a farm—which she always claimed to hate. Isn't that ironic?"

Maggie felt sorry for the woman who had lost such a fine son. "What's her husband like?"

"I've never met him. I was invited to the wedding, and both of them have urged me to come and visit, but... well, I'm pretty busy, and when I do have time for visits I go home to West Virginia to see Pap."

"Maybe you should make the effort, Tucker."

He shrugged. "Tell me about your family."

"I have four older brothers—they were practically teenagers when I was born. My parents thought their family was complete, but I was an addendum. Mother informed Dad she'd never forgive him if I turned out to be another rowdy boy.

"I've always been treated with loving indulgence by my family. That's why I was able to get my degree in fine art. They regarded my education as something to do until I snagged a husband. Now they barely seem to tolerate me living alone in Sallyville, so far from the nest. I think they're a little disappointed in me. Only one daughter and she turns out to be defective. As far as they're concerned the least I could do is move back to Ekalaka and teach art like any self-respecting spinster would have done by now."

"I don't think you qualify for spinsterhood quite yet," Tucker disagreed, eyeing her provocatively before adding, "I'd say you had a couple of good years left on you before you start deteriorating."

Maggie elbowed him. "Thanks a heap. You're as bad as they are. Every time I go home they line me up with a local husband candidate. It's horrible."

"I know what you mean." Tucker laughed. "My partner, John Baker, and his wife are always inviting me to dinner when someone's long-lost fourth cousin just happens to be passing through. I don't think married people can stand to see anyone happier apart than they are together."

"I don't believe that at all. I think they want the people they love to have a life as full and rewarding as their own."

Uh-oh. This woman wouldn't mind having a husband at all. And Tucker decided that was one more reason to be thankful he'd come to his senses before things had gone too far. "So," he asked to fill the tense silence, "what kind of man are you looking for? In a husband?"

Maggie considered. "I'm not exactly out to snare a husband, but I think it would be important that we enjoy doing the same things."

"What sort of things?"

"Moonlight walks in the park or along the lake," she answered dreamily.

"I've never been that adventurous. Walking in the park can be dangerous at night," Tucker said matter-of-factly.

"That's what I like about small towns—they're safe and friendly. I'd want us to raise our family in a small town."

Miss Mousey rides again. Next she'd tell him she wanted tons of children. "So you and Mr. Right will live in a small town and have two-point-three kids, huh?"

"I've never been average. I want a large family. Several children."

He knew it! He'd have to watch his step with this one for sure. He wouldn't even consider seeing her again when this was all over. And he would have to keep a distance between them during this forced alliance. So what was he doing in the same bed with her?

"What other qualifications are you looking for?" The more she talked about marriage, the easier it might be to keep that distance.

"It would be nice if he liked classical music." She ticked her forefinger.

Yuck.

She moved on to the next finger. "I love seafood and it's something I enjoy cooking, even if I was born miles from the ocean."

Tucker grimaced; he was allergic to shellfish.

Maggie was really getting warmed up now. "Oh, yes, he should definitely have a background in the arts."

He pursued his lips thoughtfully. Thank goodness whittling was considered a craft, not an art. "Why?"

She grinned impishly. "So we would have something to talk about after we put all those kids to bed."

The homey image of Maggie and some faceless art lover settling down to domesticity made Tucker peevish. "Hey, that's not a bad idea, because you're going to need something to talk about to keep from nodding off. The two of you will probably bore each other to death in two weeks."

"What a nasty thing to say. I was merely pointing out some qualities that I find attractive in a man."

Qualities that were conspicuously absent in him, Tucker noted. "You keep those qualifications in mind, you're going to end up shackled to a nerd for the rest of your life." What did he care? he wondered. Why was he getting in such a fizz? It was nothing to him if Maggie Ryan ended up with a dud for a husband.

"You'll probably wind up living with a barmaid somewhere," she countered. "And without the benefit of matrimony so that you'll be free to pick up and leave when the going gets rough."

"You don't know anything about me, Maggie. I was merely pointing out that a man like you described would be no match for you. I think you need someone to spark the vitality you keep hidden away. You're so...so...rigid."

"Rigid?" Maggie had to take two deep breaths before she could speak without raising her voice. She recalled the redhead he had flirted with in Tingle's. Clearly that was his type of woman. "Maybe I just seem stiff to you because you're so loose. Why, Mata Hari would probably seem tame to you."

"I only meant that you should have a man who would help bring you out of yourself. You don't seem to live your life to the fullest. You aren't nearly as dull as you seem, you know." Tucker watched her face set, fascinated by the twitching muscle in her left jaw. Maybe he had gone too far; he should have left out that last bit.

"Now I'm dull. Thank you so much for all your kind words. I suppose if I was a barmaid you'd feel more attracted to me yourself and you wouldn't be calling me dull. In fact, we probably would have made love by now and you'd have rolled over and gone right to sleep, like a...contented...pig."

"That's ridiculous!" he bellowed. He wouldn't have gone *right* to sleep. Not with her. "You seem to have a real fixation about barmaids. They do a job like everyone else, so what do you have against them?"

"I don't have anything against them in general." It was just one red-haired one in particular that had upset her so much. "I should have made it clear that my contempt is for the type of woman you were carrying on with at Tingle's, and she just happened to be a barmaid."

"Carrying on?" he parroted.

"You were grinning at her like an idiot, you winked at her like there was a boulder in your eye, and you squirreled that money into her bosom like it was acorns to last the winter."

"Well, well, well. Ms. Prim-and-Proper's completely back now. I guess you've gotten over your fright and once again you're the same old ho-hum person I suspected you were." He couldn't seem to stop the angry words even though he knew he was hurting her, goading her beyond reasonable limits. But the injustice of it was lost in the heat of the moment.

"Ooooh," Maggie squealed. "Ooooh." If her right hand weren't locked to the bed, she hated to think what she might do to him. "I'd like to punch your lights out, you...you..." She plopped down on the bed, covering her head with her pillow.

Never in her whole life had she called a man such a vile name as the one that had come to her mind. And never, never had she been tempted to do anyone bodily harm. And never, never, never had she wanted a man to take her in his arms as much as she wanted J. P. Tucker to take her. Damn. Damn. Damn.

"Go on, say it. I've been called a bastard before, you know. It wouldn't be the first time." Tucker clicked off the light and lay down, sorry that he'd said those ugly things to her. She was a nice girl and she didn't deserve it. Hell, he just wasn't used to dealing with nice women. He was thirty-four years old and he didn't want to start at this late date.

He turned his back to her. No. He wasn't going to start something he had no intention of finishing—not with Maggie Ryan. He closed his eyes and willed sleep to overcome him, but he couldn't help wondering if his refusal to get involved with her was because he knew his intentions were dishonorable, or because he knew he would never get enough of her?

Chapter Five

Maggie's eyes were red and swollen when Tucker ushered her into the coffee shop adjoining the motel the next morning. And that made him mad at himself and impatient with her as a result. "Why are you carrying that damned poke?" he asked when she set the brown bag on the table in their booth.

"Poke? Is that what you call sacks in West Virginia?"

Tucker grinned. "Sack? Is that what you call pokes in Montana?"

Maggie smiled although she wouldn't have thought it possible after last night. "To answer your first question, I've substituted this *poke* for my purse. It's got all my stuff in it."

Tucker groaned. "We wouldn't want to lose any of your valuables, would we?"

"I also have your toothbrush and the razor you left in the bathroom," she reminded him.

He rubbed his raw cheek where he'd shaved with soap and the unfamiliar disposable razor. "We can get more toothbrushes."

Maggie had insisted that he put the cuffs on her and go out to the vending machine in the hall for toilet articles this morning, refusing to step a foot out the door until she'd brushed her teeth. He'd complied with her request for the cuffs only because he didn't want her to think he was going soft. He still had some reservations about her.

Sometime during the night he'd wrapped her in his arms when he'd heard her crying. He had held her tenderly, muttering soothing words that he didn't care to remember in the harsh light of day, and then they'd finally slept. Just slept, that was all. But it had been the sweetest experience of his life. Tucker wasn't sure he could endure another night like that—he had to get rid of her somehow.

But Peterson had been adamant when Tucker had called him earlier. They were to go straight to a nearby town and pick up the money wired there in his name. He had further orders not to return with Maggie to D.C. until Peterson deemed it safe to do so.

Tucker privately wondered what all the cloak-and-dagger stuff was about. The usual procedure was to place a witness under guard in a safe house. The guys from the warehouse had not been picked up, but Tucker couldn't imagine them presenting much of a problem and he couldn't figure out why he had been ordered to lie low. But then, he reasoned, he didn't get paid to figure, he got paid to follow orders and that's what he would do.

Maggie's interruption prevented him from exploring his thoughts further. "You said you were running out of money, and I consider a toothbrush a necessity." She patted the sack fondly before adding, "Since I lost my purse, I need this. It gives me a sense of security."

The waitress stood at their table, and it irritated Maggie that she was giving Tucker a knowledgeable once-over. "What'll it be?"

"I'll have bacon, eggs, grits, biscuits and gravy and a glass of orange juice." Tucker gave his order without consulting the menu. Then with a grin that Maggie felt was unnecessarily flirty, he added, "And lots of black coffee while I'm waiting."

"You got it," the waitress said with a wink.

And you'd like to get it, Maggie thought uncharitably as she studied her plastic-coated menu.

"What about you, Maggie?" Tucker prompted impatiently.

"I'll have toast and grapefruit juice, please."

When the waitress swayed her hips back to the window to place their orders, Tucker couldn't resist saying, "We aren't broke yet. You should have ordered a proper breakfast."

"Proper breakfast?" Maggie echoed. "You're eating yourself into an early grave with all that cholesterol, not to mention the carbohydrates. How can you eat that stuff?"

"I'm hungry. As you recall, we didn't get to finish our dinner." Now why had he brought that up?

Maggie didn't care to think about *why* they'd interrupted their meal, so she glanced around the café, embarrassed. The place was motel typical—tile floor, chrome tables, vinyl booths. At the front was a counter with stools where a few truck drivers hunched over their food.

Not wanting to look at Tucker, who was even more devastating in the daylight, Maggie chose to stare out the window. Absently she noted the blazing autumn colors of the trees crowding the asphalt parking lot, the russet and yellow chrysanthemums in tubs on either side of the motel office door. Then she noticed something that was strangely out of place in the peaceful setting.

"Tucker, see that dark car parked at the motel office?"

His eyes narrowed in alarm when he recognized it. "Looks like the same car, doesn't it? We've got to get out of here." He'd have to get a look at the plates to be sure, but there was no need to take chances.

"Yes. But that car's blue and I thought the one at the warehouse was black." Maggie took another look at the car in question.

"Let's go, Maggie." Tucker stood as the waitress piled their plates on the table. He handed her a bill. "Thanks, but we've changed our minds."

"What am I supposed to do with all this food?" she demanded, arms akimbo.

Filled with inspiration, Maggie opened her sack and dumped the bacon and biscuits inside. "Oh, we'll just have it to go, won't we, darling? My husband is eager to get on with the honeymoon." She downed her juice in one gulp as the waitress and Tucker stared in openmouthed surprise. "You know how unpredictable men are," she explained airily as Tucker grabbed her by the hand and yanked her out the door.

Here we go again, Tucker thought as they got into the car and sped out of the parking lot. They were off and running and he wasn't sure why. Whose game of cat and mouse were they playing? Had that business of sending him for toothpaste been Maggie's way of stalling for time until her accomplices could get to them? Maybe she hadn't been trying to call her boss at all last night when he was in the bathroom.

But if Maggie was mixed up in this, why had she alerted him to the car? Maybe she'd changed her mind at the last minute, he reasoned. Maybe what had passed between them last night had meant something to her. No. Even though it was Tucker's nature and livelihood to be suspicious, he couldn't convince himself that Maggie was a part of anything criminal.

"How do you suppose they found us?" Maggie watched over her shoulder to make sure they weren't being followed.

"Beats me."

"Why aren't they chasing us now?"

"Dammit, I'm not psychic. I don't know." Tucker really didn't know, and that's what made him snap at her.

"I read a book once called *Cop on the Run* and the hero was being stalked by some really bad guys." She smiled triumphantly. "But I knew before the end that it was his partner who'd betrayed him."

"Well, I hate to spoil your fun, but John Baker is not only my partner but my best friend. I haven't spoken to him since Friday afternoon and he probably won't know anything about all this until he reports for duty Monday morning."

Tucker slowed to the speed limit and Maggie stared out the passenger window, watching the vibrant foliage streak by and considering his words. For the next several miles she thought about their situation and wondered if she would ever really understand why she was on the run with J. P. Tucker.

When they reached the small town Peterson had directed him to, Tucker drove to the Western Union office and parked. "I'll go in and pick up the money the department promised to wire." He felt the heavy handcuffs in his pocket and debated momentarily before deciding they were unnecessary. Orders or no orders, he'd be damned if he would lock Maggie to the steering wheel. "Sit tight and I'll be right back." If she bolted and made a run for it... at least he would finally discover where her loyalties lay.

He crossed the street and entered the small building. When he opened the door a little bell jingled to alert the person in the back that a customer was waiting. Another hick town, he sighed. He was ready to get back to D.C.

Waiting impatiently, Tucker glanced out the window and saw the guy with the gold tooth sneaking up to the passenger side of his car. Another sleazy-looking man was sneaking up on the driver's side. They were after Maggie.

Tucker wrenched open the door and ran, calling to her. "Maggie, lock the doors!"

She couldn't hear him, so she leaned across the seat and unsuspectingly pushed open the door. "What did you say?"

Tucker couldn't believe his eyes. It was happening again. Maggie was being kidnapped right out from under his nose.

Gold Tooth hauled a screaming, kicking Maggie from the car as Tucker made a flying leap to Sleazy's back, knocking him to the ground. They grappled in the street, gathering a modest host of onlookers, until Tucker landed a successful right cross to the man's jaw and ended the struggle. Like a flash, he leaped up to save Maggie.

However, Tucker wasn't sure she needed saving. Maggie fought like a wildcat, delivering a well-placed kick to Gold Tooth's most vulnerable spot. He fell to his knees, his head bent in agony. Before Tucker could intercede, Maggie locked her hands together and brought them down hard on the back of the man's neck. From Tucker's vantage point, it looked as if she knew what she was doing.

"Don't just stand there with your mouth open!" she yelled at Tucker as she sprang for the car. "Here come reinforcements."

He jumped into the driver's seat just as Tiny came barreling down on them, his gun flashing in the early-morning sunlight. They took off in a burst of speed and a shower of bullets.

Some days it just didn't pay to get out of bed.

Tucker barely had time to think as he negotiated the narrow two-lane highway out of town. But one thought, which had nagged him since they'd seen the car at the motel, intruded on his concentration. Was it possible that there was a leak within the department? That was the only way those thugs could have known his destination. But who? And more important, why? He was running out of money and he didn't know where to turn. The only person Tucker knew he could trust was John Baker, but whoever was mixed up in this was probably watching him, too.

"They're not chasing us," Maggie announced after seeing no sign of the men on the road behind them.

"They don't need to. They already know where we're going."

"What do you mean?"

"They think they do, anyway. I'm going to try and outsmart them by doubling back through these woods. I think I know where we'll be safe." Tucker pulled off the highway onto a narrow dirt track. He drove far into the heavily treed area, looking for a spot he remembered from a long-ago hunting trip.

"Why are we stopping?" Maggie's heart was still thudding painfully in her chest. She didn't know how she had found the courage to defend herself from the weasel, with actions that were clearly more Clementine than Maggie. But when she had seen that hateful face leering at her, she knew she would never allow herself to fall into his grasp again.

"I want you to go down there and get behind a tree and toss out your clothes."

Maggie's eyes widened. "Now?"

"Get your mind out of the gutter, Ms. Ryan," Tucker teased. "I just want to see if those goons planted a homing device on you back at that warehouse."

Maggie stepped out of the car and started in the direction Tucker had pointed. She paused and looked back at him doubtfully. "Everything?"

"Everything."

Later, Maggie was mad as a hornet when she got dressed. Her wardrobe, already pitifully insufficient, was now depleted by one more item—her bra. Tucker had ripped it to smithereens in a vain attempt to find the nonexistent bug.

"Do I get to return the favor?" she asked, relishing the idea of getting her hands on his Art Deco underwear.

"I'll do it myself; I know what to look for." To be thorough, Tucker decided to check himself, even though the men had not really had an opportunity to plant anything on him. He walked into the screen of bushes as Maggie came out. "I'm sorry about your underwear."

"My only regret," she mumbled, "is that I have but one bra to give for my country."

Tucker chuckled. "You're priceless, Maggie."

"I'm also hungry." She got her brown bag from the car and carried it to a nearby clearing, certain that disposable handbags would never catch on.

"So am I." Tucker had finished his own body search and now sat on the ground across from her. "What have you got in that doggie bag?"

Maggie peered into the sack, looked up at him and wrinkled her nose. "A mess."

"Can you salvage any of it?"

She pulled her slip out first. "Wouldn't you know it? Grease spots are a pain to get out of tricot."

"The food, Maggie—can you salvage the food?"

She made an unlikely tablecloth of her slip and poured the contents of the bag onto it. Tucker picked up her sweater and tossed it aside, grateful at least that she'd left her other shoes at the motel.

Maggie selected a biscuit, opened it, placed crumbled pieces of bacon between the halves and handed it to Tucker. "It's all yours if you can eat it. I should have wrapped it up in napkins or something."

Tucker took the cold biscuit and bit into it before giving himself time to think where it had just spent the last two hours. "S'good," he mumbled, his mouth full of the dried-out bread.

Maggie watched him dubiously as she made a similar sandwich for herself. "Beggars can't be choosers, right?"

"Right," he agreed, wishing he had a cup of coffee to wash it down with.

"You know, I told you about *Cop on the Run*? Well, this bad guy put a homing device in his partner's car and—"

"That's it," Tucker said, snapping his fingers. "How could I be so dense? I'll go over the car while you finish eating."

If there was anything planted on the car, he couldn't find it. He'd taken apart the interior, piece by piece, and the car was now a shambles.

"I hope you can put it back together again," Maggie said hopefully.

"I could, but I'm not going to." He rolled his shirtsleeves down and put his jacket back on.

"We're just going to drive it like this?" Maggie noted with dismay that the seats had been incongruously tossed under a nearby tree like lawn chairs at a salvage yard.

"No. I couldn't find anything, but that's no sign there isn't a bug in there somewhere. Besides, it's nearly out of gas and probably wouldn't even get us back to the main highway."

"We're leaving it here?"

"That's the plan."

"Where are we going to get another car way out here?" Maggie asked. "Or does your superior have one stashed away in a cave or something?"

"Afraid not. We'll hike, taking the back roads. It'll be safer that way."

"You mean we're going to walk?" Maggie gasped.

"That's the common definition of hiking." Tucker made a big production of picking up Maggie's meager possessions, placing them inside her slip and tying the whole thing into a huge knot. "Want me to find you a long stick so you can carry this over your shoulder like a hobo?"

"Tucker, I think I should tell you right off that I do not want to do this. In fact," Maggie emphasized, flopping onto one of the displaced car seats, "I'm *not* going to do it."

"There's no alternative. If we stay with the car, they'll find us. Walking is the only way we're going to get out of here."

"Are you positive? Are we really in that much danger?"

"Yes to both questions. I'm sorry, but it's the only way."

"I'm probably going to be a real gripe. I'm not a physical person," Maggie moaned.

"How can you say that to the guy who just saw you beat up that punk back there?"

"That was just a reaction—glands or something." She smiled wistfully. "I was pretty tough, though, wasn't I?"

"The toughest."

"Still, that was an extraordinary circumstance. I'm a natural born klutz most of the time."

"You'll do fine. A little walk is good for you now and then. You can just pretend you're out for a stroll in the park, or along the lake with your ideal man, remember?"

"Sure." They lit out, and Maggie wondered if the snakes had gone into hibernation yet. There was no impenetrable undergrowth in any of the parks Maggie had ever strolled through, in her fantasies or otherwise. Tucker took her arm to prevent her from stumbling over a large root, and his touch was almost her undoing.

"I think we've passed by here before," she muttered after they had lumbered along in silence for hours.

"No, we haven't. You've just got a lousy sense of direction for a country girl."

"It's not *my* sense of direction I'm worried about. You're leading the way," Maggie muttered pessimistically.

"Don't they have woods in Montana? Didn't your brothers ever take you camping? Just pretend you're on a camping trip," Tucker encouraged, trying to make her forget that night was closing in fast and the woods would soon be totally dark.

"Yes, there are woods in Montana, and yes, I've gone camping before. In a Winnebago. Mom and I played

Scrabble in air-conditioned comfort while Dad and the guys made like Grizzly Adams.'' She looked around. When had it grown so dark? A few moments ago she'd watched the sun setting behind the crimson and gold treetops and thought how beautiful it was.

Now, doubt and fear nagged her mercilessly. The growing darkness fueled her imagination and it ran rampant, spurred on by the throbbing chorus of night sounds. The path grew narrower, then disappeared completely, and Maggie felt surrounded by trees and dense undergrowth. The gnarled, sparsely leafed limbs seemed to reach out and grab at the sweater she had donned when the pale crescent moon had changed places with the sun. Surely this dark, evil-looking path could have been traveled by Ichabod Crane when he fled the headless horseman.

The sudden, nearby hooting of an owl sent her flying into Tucker's protective arms. ''Don't worry, Maggie. Trust me,'' he soothed. ''I'll have us out of here in no time.''

Chapter Six

No time? Try never.

They wandered around the gloomy forest until Maggie was cross and irritable. She had to pick her way over windfalls, around exposed roots and through drifts of moldy leaves. With each floundering step she silently railed at the circumstances that had brought her to such a pass. None of the events of the past twenty-four hours made any sense at all.

Finally, when she could go no farther, Maggie plopped down on a moss-covered log. "I refuse to go another step. I deserve an explanation of why I'm being dragged around this godforsaken forest and I want it now. Who are those gun-toting thugs and what do they want with me?"

Taking in her resolute look, Tucker sat down beside her. He knew she wouldn't be satisfied with the information he was at liberty to give her, but at this point he had to operate on a need-to-know basis. "If I told you everything you might be in even more danger. Can't you trust me enough to let me handle this? Let me take care of you?"

Maggie took off a running shoe that had long ago conformed to the shape of someone else's foot and threw it on the ground. "I guess so," she said grudgingly. "You got me into this mess. I have no choice but to trust you to get me out of it."

Tucker stood and implored the darkening heavens. "*I* got you into it?" he beseeched. "You're the one who had to go and get yourself kidnapped. I was perfectly willing to watch you waste your dreary little life with nothing better to do than read. But no, you had to go out cruising for men—"

"I was *not* cruising for men!"

"Well, what would you call it?"

"I don't call it anything. I went dancing with a friend."

"Same thing. What's the difference?"

Maggie took off her other shoe and flung it in the general direction of its mate. "I don't have to explain anything to you."

"No, you don't. But I refuse to let you blame me. I didn't get you tangled up with a gang of counterfeiters—you did that all by yourself."

Her head jerked up in surprise. "Counterfeiters? Is that what this is all about?" When he only nodded, Maggie sighed. "Is this the part you don't want to tell me?"

"I can't, Maggie."

"So don't." She'd had an idea and was intent on executing it.

Tucker watched as Maggie gathered bits of dried wood, then cleared leaves out of a circle on the ground. "What are you doing?"

"I'm ignoring you. I'm going to build myself a fire because I'm cold." She collected a few stones to place around the edge and was satisfied that it resembled every picture she had ever seen of a well-laid camp fire, even if her brothers hadn't seen fit to teach her the finer points of woodlore.

Tucker sat down beside her. "We can't build a fire, Maggie," he said softly.

"I don't care what you say. I've had it. I don't care if every kidnapper, counterfeiter and highwayman in the country sees my little flames. I'm cold! Besides, they aren't all that great at their job, and I don't think they're physically up to a great deal of walking, which is the only way they could possibly get to us now. It's my bet they're holed up in some sleazy—but *warm*—hotel. Give me a match, Tucker."

He shook his head slowly from side to side. "I'm sorry."

Maggie suddenly grabbed him by the front of his leather jacket, inwardly appalled by the aggressive feelings that washed over her. The sound that came out of her was that of a small but desperate animal. "Give me a match," she ground out.

"I can't do that, Maggie."

She clutched his jacket tighter, and with her last ounce of leashed control, she demanded, "Give me a damn match."

Tucker began to laugh, and Maggie shook him, yelling, "It isn't funny, damn you!" He toppled back onto the leafy ground and Maggie went with him, straddling him as he lay laughing like a loon. "I'm not responsible, Tucker," she screeched as her fists pounded against his chest. "Give me a match!"

Tucker grasped her flailing hands, rolled over and pinned her to the ground. "I don't have any matches," he explained between gasping bouts of hilarity.

His laughter was the last straw. Maggie felt the cascading tears before she could stop them. What was the matter with her? A gentle person by nature, she had resorted to force. Obviously it was the act of a desperate person.

Tucker lay down beside her in the crinkly leaves and gently gathered her into his arms. "Don't cry, Maggie. Please," he begged, softly, his lips against her temple.

Maggie hiccupped. "I don't know what came over me," she sobbed. "I've never done anything like this before. I'm so tired."

"I know," he whispered consolingly. "I swear we'll find the road as soon as it's light in the morning. I'm sure I heard traffic somewhere."

"That wasn't traffic," she sniffed. "It was one lousy car."

He stroked her back. "Whatever. But I know I heard tires singing. There has to be a road nearby."

"But where?" she wailed.

"I promise you, I'll find it in the morning."

"Ohh," she groaned. "Morning? I'll be frozen by then and you'll need a truck with a winch to haul me out of these boonies."

Tucker grinned and tickled her dimple. "Was that a little joke, Maggie? Is that the beginnings of a smile? Hmm? Is it?" he teased, his face inching closer with each question.

Maggie bit her lip, trying to keep the grin from bursting through. How did he do it? He could incite her to violence one minute, and have her grinning like an idiot the next. "I'm sorry I hit you. But you were laughing at me."

"I know and I'm sorry. Just when I thought you were going to rub two sticks together, you asked me for a match. How could I not laugh? I tried to tell you I didn't have any."

"But I worked so hard to get it just right," she said, bemoaning the still-cold fire pit.

"Smokey the Bear would be very proud of the camp fire you laid," he comforted.

"Gosh, I'm hungry."

"Me too."

"Tucker, somehow that's not much of a consolation. You've got a gun—go kill us something for dinner."

"It's getting too dark."

"Don't all those little furry critters come out at night?"

"Maybe. But even if I accidentally got something, we'd have to eat it raw. No matches, remember?"

"Oh, yeah."

"Try to think of something else, Maggie."

"Okay," she complied. "I'm cold, too."

He chuckled as he wrapped her tightly in the circle of his arms and legs. "That I can do something about. Put your arms around me, Maggie." When she hesitated, he added, "Purely for survival purposes." He knew that was a dumb statement and it wouldn't take long for her to recognize it for the lie it really was. As close as they were lying, she couldn't miss it. To get his mind off the proximity of Maggie's soft body, Tucker began to mentally list all the presidents since George Washington. In order.

By the time Maggie slid her hands inside his jacket, wrapped her arms around his waist and snuggled against his chest, he'd gotten up to Millard Fillmore but it wasn't helping.

"Ouch."

"What's the matter?" he asked.

"That bazooka strapped to your body is a little uncomfortable."

"Sorry." Tucker sat up and removed his shoulder holster. Once more wound tightly in each other's arms, he asked huskily, "How's that?"

Maggie wriggled closer to his warm body, which fairly radiated heat. "Much better. I feel toasty now, except for my feet."

"Put them between my legs," he suggested.

"Purely for survival purposes?"

"Certainly."

"Mmm. That's terrific. You must have an inner pilot light or something, huh?"

"Or something," he muttered. "Be still now and go to sleep."

"Okay." She yawned. "But first I'd like to thank you for putting up with me. I know it hasn't been easy for you."

"It hasn't been so bad. I feel partly to blame for some of the things that have happened to you. I don't deserve your thanks."

Maggie sighed and cuddled into his chest. It was so pleasant lying in Tucker's arms that she could almost forget their difficult circumstances. The animal sounds of the woods no longer unnerved her, and the deepening night was no longer fearsome. She wondered idly if Tucker had any other good survival techniques. "You know what, Tucker? You're turning out to be a nice guy, after all."

"Aw, shucks, ma'am," he bantered. "Being a nice guy was never one of my intentions."

Maggie giggled. "Guess what, Tucker?"

"What, Maggie?"

"At the risk of spoiling the mood, I'm going to say something stupid. I'm afraid I'm beginning to like you." What she was really afraid of was that she was beginning to *more* than like him.

"Oh, no," he gasped dramatically. "Not that." He was beginning to like her, too, and that was scary to a man who felt that ordering home newspaper delivery was too permanent a commitment.

Maggie closed her eyes and settled down, wondering what Holly would say if she could see her now. "Tucker..."

There wasn't room for a sweet, caring woman in his life, and even if there were Tucker wouldn't know how to handle her. "Hush, Legs. Get some rest. We have some heavy-duty walking to do tomorrow."

"Where are we going?" she asked sleepily.

"Somewhere safe."

The sun did come up eventually, but its feeble warmth was ineffective in ridding Tucker and Maggie of the bone-deep chill that had settled over them during the night. Tucker dragged an aching Maggie to her feet and they set out in the direction, they hoped, of the elusive highway.

"My feet hurt, I'm hungry and I'm tired," Maggie complained after a while.

"Gripe, gripe, gripe, that's all I've heard for the past five miles. I'm tired, too. And did I or did I not find breakfast for us?" Tucker wanted to know.

"Yes, you certainly did. How could I have forgotten those delectable persimmons. I haven't puckered so much since I worked the kissing booth at the Senior Citizens' Bazaar last year."

"After a couple of more frosts we could come back here and eat those and you'd think you'd died and gone to heaven," he replied knowingly.

"You should be ashamed of yourself for mentioning dying to a starving person, Tucker. It's rude."

"I beg your pardon. How can you be starving? You ate most of the walnuts I found. And we wouldn't have had any lunch at all if I hadn't insisted that you save some of them for later."

"True, there was nothing wrong with the walnuts," Maggie agreed. "What there was of them."

"And who nearly broke his back letting you stand on his shoulders to shake the damned things loose?"

"You did. But you didn't hold me up long enough to get all I wanted."

"Something tells me you'd never get all you wanted," Tucker griped. "And you're a lot heavier than you look," he added, quickly sidestepping her elbow.

"Well, hang around. At the rate we're going I'll be a lot thinner in no time at all."

Tucker knew he had to get her mind off food. "I found the road this morning, too, just as I promised."

Maggie clamped her hands on the small of her back and attempted to stretch out some of the soreness. "No doubt we almost stumbled over it a hundred times in the dark last night."

"Listen," Tucker breathed, cupping his hand to his ear. "Do you hear anything?"

"Just my stomach rumbling."

"Wait, I'm sure I heard an engine."

"Engine, shmengine. I'd be happy to see a passing horse and buggy." Maggie sank onto a log away from the edge of the road and patted it invitingly. "You'd better sit down and rest. The rush-hour traffic will be starting up soon and you'll need all your energy to stand there and hold out your thumb."

Tucker joined her. "If we wait here long enough, someone is sure to come along." He stared down the empty road that seemed to stretch endlessly in both directions.

"Tucker?"

"Hmm?"

"Could there have been a nuclear attack that we don't know about?"

"Don't be ridiculous."

"I read a book about a couple of lovers who went camping for a weekend and when they came back everyone was gone." Maggie snapped her fingers. "Phfft! Just like that. Civilization as they knew it had been wiped from the face of the earth."

"This isn't a book, Maggie," Tucker pointed out. And they weren't lovers, he didn't point out. "It isn't a movie, it's real life. The world is still out there somewhere; we just have to find it." He didn't mention that it seemed weird to him that they hadn't seen a living soul on the road all day. Being alone with her was beginning to corrode his brain.

"If you say so," she said patronizingly.

Tucker rolled his eyes.

"Listen!" Maggie cried. "It's a car!" She jumped to her feet and ran to the edge of the road.

"It's an engine, that's for sure," Tucker agreed as they both turned expectantly, jubilantly, toward the longed-for sound.

A black-clad creature with goggle eyes, long hair flying behind him like a banner, hurtled past like a meteor—just as spectacular and just as short-lived.

Tucker slapped his thigh in frustration. "Damn!"

"Hey, you!" Maggie screamed after the motorcyclist. "Are there any survivors up ahead?" Then she turned to Tucker with her own frustrated anger. "Why'd you let him get away?"

"What would you have me do?" he asked snidely. "Trip him? Shoot him? Maybe he would have stopped if you'd rolled up your pant legs."

"Maybe he would have," Maggie said, pouting.

They sat on the log in dejected silence for a moment, then Maggie began to chuckle. "Okay, Tucker. You've been holding out on me long enough. It's time for the secret weapons."

"What secret weapons?" He frowned, unamused.

"Your watch. Doesn't it conceal a two-way radio?"

"Sorry. It's just an ordinary digital."

"I know! Take off your shoe."

"No." He frowned again, then took the bait. "Why?"

"Doesn't it open up and turn cleverly into a telephone so we can call headquarters?"

Tucker grinned in spite of his resolve. "I'm afraid not."

"I thought those things were standard government issue."

"I'm with the Treasury Department, not the CIA, Maggie."

"CIA, FBI, IRS. What's the difference?"

"Listen, I hear something."

"I don't." Maggie stared up the road, then behind her down the same lonely stretch they'd been traveling all day. At first she didn't see it. Then she spied something at the crest of a distant hill. It was the sun glinting off the chrome of an old but highly polished pickup truck. "Tucker!" she cried. "We're saved."

An unfamiliar warmth sparked inside Tucker as he stared at Maggie's joyous expression. She jumped up and down in her excitement, and his eyes were drawn to her unfettered breasts as they moved out of synch with the rest of her body. When she threw her arms around his neck and pressed them against him, he simply forgot everything else.

He kissed her.

When her lips opened invitingly to his, Tucker felt that he'd waited ages to hold her, to touch her. He knew a distinct sense of well-being and then a wave of strong desire. Maggie's hands threaded through his hair and her slender body molded perfectly to his. Her mouth was warm and sweet to his exploring tongue, the flesh of her back silk beneath his hands as they slid under her T-shirt. The heady scents of October enveloped them in a cloud that joined with Maggie's kittenlike purrs to spiral Tucker's passion higher and higher.

Maggie was manna to a hungry man, and Tucker desperately needed more of her to satisfy his terrible craving. Never in his life had he felt such yearning, such simple yet barbaric and boundless need. He had to get close to her, so close nothing could separate the two halves of the whole they made.

His kiss was urgent and exploratory, filling Maggie's senses with a starry dizziness. She loved the gentle warmth of his hands on her skin, which tingled under his fingertips. She exulted in the knowledge that the attraction she felt for him was mutual, and consuming.

He ground his hips against hers and moved closer. Maggie moaned with the sweet agony of it. She wanted him. Only him.

At last Tucker lifted his head, breathing roughly and without rhythm, and stared down at her fascinating face. Her vivid eyes were jade dark with desire, and he felt himself falling more deeply under her spell. A man could learn to love those eyes.

Maggie caressed his stubbled jaw. "No one's ever made me feel that way before," she whispered wonderingly.

Tucker took a deep breath before he could speak. "Maggie, this is—"

"Pardon me for interruptin', folks, but I'as wonderin' if you'ns might be lost."

Saved by the proverbial bell.

How could he have become so besotted by a kiss? Tucker berated himself for the impulses that had overwhelmed his good sense. How could he have forgotten the truck? It took him entirely too long to push Maggie away from him and give the man an answer. "Yes, we're lost. Our car broke down yesterday."

Still somewhat bemused, Maggie stared at the newcomer, thinking he would be a natural if Hollywood ever decided to revive Pa Kettle.

"S'at a fact? You been wanderin' around without no food or nothin'?" The old man stroked his bristly chin thoughtfully. "You'ns wouldn't be revenooers, by any chance. Would you?"

"Absolutely not," Tucker hastened to reassure him. Since the repeal of Prohibition in 1933, an average of one agent a year had died under the fire of moonshiners' guns. The old man looked harmless enough, but there was no sense tempting fate. Emulating Maggie's active imagination, Tucker quickly concocted a reasonable story.

"We're honeymooners. We were on our way to Nag's Head." He draped a stiff arm around Maggie's equally stiff shoulders. "I'm J. P. Tucker and this is Maggie."

"Howdy do. I'm Pirdy Lee," he returned as the two men shook hands. Then he ran lazy eyes over Maggie. "Yep. You're newlyweds, all right. I can spot that glow a mile away."

Maggie didn't bother to point out that any residual glow was a result of having just been kissed to within an inch of her life. She let the old-timer ramble on while she tried to figure out what and where Nag's Head was. Tucker had conveniently avoided mentioning their destination to her—

no doubt his way of protecting her from the dangers of knowing too much.

"I reckon I could give you young folks a ride," he was saying. "I'm goin' right close to Nag's Head. But I'll have to make a few stops along the way."

"Thanks. That's great, isn't it, honey?" Tucker turned to Maggie with a big false smile plastered on his face.

She frowned. There was a ferocious-looking dog in the cab of the truck. It was growling malevolently, and the hair on its neck was standing up. "What about him?"

Pirdy Lee pursed his wrinkled lips. "Well, Bootsey don't much cotton to strangers. I reckon you'uns will have to ride in the back. There's blankets and some mighty fine honey dew back there to ward off the evenin' chill. That's about the best I can do fer ya."

"That's more than generous. We appreciate it." Tucker bumped Maggie with his hip.

"Oh, yes," she gushed. "Thanks ever so much."

The few stops turned out to be many, widely spread out over the countryside, along every back road imaginable. At each of the houses and buildings, Pirdy Lee took a few jugs of his "honey dew" and disappeared inside. It didn't take long for Tucker and Maggie to figure out what the honey dew really was. Moonshine.

"I can't believe I'm doing this. I'm actually riding shotgun with a moonshiner, delivering illegal whiskey," Tucker muttered from his corner of the pickup bed as they rattled over the road.

"I can't believe that vicious dog is riding up there in comfort instead of us," Maggie groused from the opposite corner. After the kiss on the road, she felt that the more distance between them the better. As much as she enjoyed it, getting close to Tucker could only lead to trouble. Big trouble.

"I reckon Pirdy Lee's known ol' Bootsey longer'n us," Tucker mimicked.

"Have you been hitting the honey dew, Tucker?" she queried.

"Just a little nip to ward off the evenin' chill." He laughed.

"Is it working?"

"Why, honey, I'm hotter'n a two-dollar pistol."

"Give me some of that stuff, then." Maggie scooted closer to accept the jug. She took a big drink of the liquid and her throat protested the action by promptly bursting into flames. She coughed and sputtered and Tucker clapped her on the back.

"You can't gulp this stuff like lemonade. You start slowly by taking a tiny, quick sip. Let me show you." He crooked his forefinger through the handle, propped the jug on his shoulder and swigged. "Ahh," he breathed. "Pirdy Lee knows his honey dew, all right. Try again, Maggie."

She complied and this time the liquor didn't burn quite as badly as before, her nerves having been severely damaged in the first assault. "Whoooee. I do feel warmer—it's working already."

"Yeah," Tucker agreed. "This is great stuff. You can give it to kids with bad tonsils and they disappear."

"The kids?" Maggie giggled.

"Nah, the bad tonsils. White lightning is powerful stuff," he said reverently.

She tried to frown but it turned into a grin. "Tch, tch. And you an agent of the U.S. Treasury."

"That's a different branch. I'm in counterfeiting, you know."

"Yes," she answered gloomily. "I know."

"Tell you what, Maggie," he said.

"What?" This time when she tipped the jug she noticed the fiery liquid no longer burned at all but actually had a most appealing flavor.

"I've decided to take the night off. I don't even want to think about my job. What do you think of that?"

Maggie fortified herself with another small gulp of the potion. "What? No handcuffs?"

"We didn't need them last night, did we?" Tucker took the jug and turned it up.

"No, we didn't." Her face grew warm, and she knew the firewater wasn't totally responsible. She accepted the jug Tucker passed back. Last night she had been a most willing prisoner.

The truck hit a bump and Tucker watched the liquid spill over Maggie's lips. He longed to taste it there, to help himself to the lips that were more intoxicating than any mere hundred-proof corn liquor. He dug the cuffs out of his pocket and flung them from the bumpy pickup as it rattled down the hillside.

Maggie gasped. "What did you do that for?"

"Because when I hold you, I want you to know that I'm not doing so under duress. And if you stay with me, it will be of your own free will."

Maggie took another swift sip and passed the moonshine to Tucker. "I *have* been staying with you of my own free will. I don't know why, but from the first moment, I've trusted you. I shouldn't tell you this, but last night was special for me."

"Special. Yes, that's the word for it. I shouldn't tell you *this*, but since we're playing 'fess-up,' I'm going to." He chugged again before handing it to Maggie. "I wanted to do a million unspeakable things to you last night. And again this morning. I would have, too, right there in the middle of that lonely road, if Pirdy Lee hadn't come along."

"A million, huh?" Maggie couldn't look at him, so afraid was she of what his eyes might reveal. She lay down and gazed at the first stars of evening. "I'm afraid my count wasn't quite that high, but then I don't have your experience."

Tucker stretched out beside her and slanted onto one elbow, turning her face up to his. "Do you know what you're saying?"

"Yes. I think I'd like you to do those unspeakable things, J. P. Tucker. It could be a broadening experience."

"You'd be sorry later," he said in an odd, gentle tone.

"Are you that bad?" she teased with mock seriousness.

"I've never been any good at relationships. I never enter into anything but brief encounters, and I always make sure the woman knows that in advance. It wouldn't be fair to you because I can't promise you anything tonight." He kissed her forehead gently. "And you're a woman who needs a promise."

"Yes," she mumbled sadly, realizing the truth of his words. "I think you're right."

Tucker took a deep breath and smiled, but the humor didn't quite reach his eyes. His voice was strangely uneven when he asked, "Want another drink, Legs?"

"No," Maggie said around the lump in her throat. She felt an ineffable sense of loss, as though she had come close to something wonderful but had let it slip through her fingers at the last moment. "But I would like another kiss to remind me of what I'll be missing."

"I'm not one for flogging myself, but I don't have any willpower where you're concerned. My control is shot to hell every time I touch you." Tucker's finger tenderly outlined her lips.

"You don't think we should risk it, then? Even for experimental purposes? I could always change my mind."

"I'm not sure I want you to. What if we went too far, Maggie? I'd feel so guilty."

"I promise not to let Daddy or any of my brothers hold a shotgun to your back. And Pirdy Lee and Bootsey are just a yell away if I get too amorous for you," she said playfully. "How far could we possibly go in the back of this bucking vehicle?"

Too far, he thought. "Are you sure?"

"All I want is one measly little kiss," she said with a pout.

"You've got it," he breathed against her lips.

Maggie's heart began to hammer as his mouth opened boldly over hers. His hands slid intimately over her back, her hips, molding her tightly to his muscular frame. She felt the intensity of his desire and wrapped her arms around his neck, shamelessly returning the kiss.

She gloried in the feel of his tongue parting her lips, delving into her mouth, then slowly retreating only to delve again in a wildly exciting rhythm so suggestive that she could nearly imagine the beauty of his body delving into hers.

Tucker groaned when she squirmed provocatively against him. The blood sang through his body, his bones dissolved and the backs of his knees tingled. He'd never known such wanting, such pure unadulterated need. His hands roved over her worshipfully, stroking a path across her shoulders, along the sides of her breasts, down her back until he cupped her buttocks and pulled her more tightly against him.

He released her lips, placing hot little kisses on her eyes, her cheek, her jaw and finally nuzzled her neck with gentle love bites.

"I warned you," he mumbled against her skin. "But you wouldn't listen to me. I want you."

Maggie cupped his face in her hands and pulled his head away, gazing deep into the dark eyes of the only man she would ever love. Love? When had that happened? How had it happened? Amazing as it was, Maggie knew she loved Tucker, knew it with as much certainty as she knew her own name. "I know," she breathed. "I know."

As if they lived beneath the solemn protection of the gods, Pirdy Lee chose that exact moment to pound exuberantly against the side of his truck. "This is as far as we go, folks."

It damned well wasn't far enough, Tucker thought as he extricated himself from Maggie's arms and helped her out the back. "Thanks, Pirdy. Let me give you something for your trouble,'' he offered as they met the man halfway around the side of the truck.

''T'weren't no trouble at all. I was comin' this far, anyways. You just save your money—you'll be needin' it. Seein' as how you're just startin' out and all.''

''Thank you. I don't know what would have happened to us if you hadn't given us a ride,'' Maggie said.

The old man seemed embarrassed by their gratitude. ''There's a store 'bout haffa mile up the road,'' he said, pointing south. He leaned over the truck bed and handed Tucker a brand-new crock of his honey dew. ''Take this,'' he said, holding up a halting hand when Tucker tried to protest. ''It'll come in handy on a long cold night. My little weddin' present to the both of you.''

Tucker was getting antsy with Pirdy Lee's talk of weddings and starting-outs and long cold nights, so he took Maggie's hand and pulled her behind him in the direction Pirdy had pointed. ''Pleasure meeting you, Pirdy Lee,'' he called over his shoulder.

''We'll never forget your kindness. So long,'' Maggie added.

She trudged along behind Tucker, wondering what would happen next. Could she have a short, meaningful relationship with him? Could she *not*? He'd already told her he couldn't make any promises. Did she want any? Did she need any? Yes, God help her, she did. But only from J. P. Tucker. How she loved the man.

''Tucker?''

''What?''

''What does J.P. stand for?''

''I'm not going to tell you,'' he said, thinking that he had to keep some secrets safe from this woman who could probe his very soul. He'd already confided too much, betraying far too much of himself to her, opening himself up for inevitable pain.

He had no intention of letting this thing get any further out of hand than it already had.

Chapter Seven

Nag's Head, a small fishing community situated on a narrow spit of land off the northern coast of North Carolina, was just south of Kitty Hawk and Kill Devil Hills. From May to Labor Day it bustled with tourists and summer people who inhabited the many houses built on stilts over the sand dunes.

"This time of year, only the year-round residents stay, and that's why most of the houses are dark," Tucker explained as they walked up the road. "It's a hard place to winter because the storm-force winds nearly swamp the peninsula."

"You mean hurricanes?"

At Maggie's worried look he was quick to reassure her. "It's a bit early in the season to start battening down the hatches."

Although it was dark, with only a wan slice of moon to light their way, Maggie knew the sea was near. The sharp scent of the ocean was in the air and the faint sound of breakers rolling into shore could be heard on the still night air. To Maggie, who was from the hill country of Montana and had never seen an ocean, the smells and sounds were exotic ones.

"How much farther now, Tucker?" she asked.

"The store's just ahead, so we'll stop and pick up a few things before going on to Mark's beach house."

"Are you sure your friend won't mind us staying there?" she inquired dubiously.

"I told you, the welcome mat's always out. Mark and I go back a long ways."

"So you have the key, then?"

"Not exactly."

The lights of the store beckoned them, and Maggie had never been so glad to see signs of civilization. She hoped a few of the "things" Tucker had promised to pick up included a change of clothing and some shampoo. She could think of nothing more satisfying than washing her hair. And it would be great to sleep in a bed again; it seemed like months since she'd left Sallyville with Holly.

Holly. What must her friend be thinking? It had been more than forty-eight hours since Maggie had stepped out of Tingle's for some fresh air. Holly was surely worried and had probably turned in a missing-persons report by now. Maggie hoped she had not called her parents. She hated the thought of them being distressed needlessly.

"Tucker? When we get to the store, may I call my friend and let her know I'm all right?"

He hesitated. It wouldn't be a good idea for anyone to know their whereabouts just yet. Not until he had time to figure this thing out. "You have to promise not to reveal where you are. Okay?"

That was no big problem. Maggie didn't really know where she was herself. "Okay."

They entered the old-fashioned general store and Tucker positioned himself near the public telephone in order to overhear Maggie's side of the conversation. It wasn't that he didn't trust her. Of course he trusted her. It was just that it was his job to be cautious, and being cautious meant keeping his ear to the ground. Or to the phone, as the case might be. He pretended to be absorbed in judging the relative merits of Swiss cheese versus Gouda so that Maggie wouldn't suspect he was eavesdropping.

"Holly? It's Maggie.... I'm all right.... No.... Yes.... It's a long story that I can't tell you at the moment.... I don't know, a few days, maybe more.... Look, Holly, just take it easy. It's nothing like that.... No! I did *not* get lucky...well, sort of, yes.... I'll let you know when I get home.... I'm glad you didn't call my parents.... Don't worry, I'm in good hands.... I just can't say, but I'll be home soon.... Bye."

Tucker could well imagine the other side of the conversation. Maggie's friend seemed like the type who would naturally assume a man had to be involved somehow. And she would be right. He picked the Swiss and sauntered to a shelf containing boxes of crackers.

"Did you get an earful?" Maggie asked at his elbow.

"I beg your pardon?"

"Don't play innocent with me, Tucker. I saw you eavesdropping. You didn't have to do that; you should have just asked what we were talking about."

"Okay. What did she say?"

"None of your business," Maggie said airily as she looked in dismay at his purchases. "Is that all we're going to have to eat? Cheese and crackers?"

"You worry more about your stomach than anyone I've ever known."

"It's only been since I met you that my stomach has required any worry." She looked at the cheese and grimaced. "At least it's not persimmons."

"I thought I'd get some Fig Newtons and beer, too." Tucker grinned when Maggie's nose wrinkled further in distaste.

"I'd like some hot soup and shampoo."

"That doesn't sound too appetizing. One of your specialties?"

She glared at him before spinning around and marching to the cosmetics counter, where she gazed wistfully at the limited assortment of lipstick, mascara and moisturizing lotions. There was something comforting about once again being in a world where such items existed. She'd had enough of the back-to-nature movement to last the rest of her life.

"We don't have enough money to waste any of it on junk like that," Tucker said behind her.

"I wasn't planning to waste any of your precious money. I just wanted to look. Is there any crime in looking?" she wanted to know.

"None that I've ever heard of."

"Then go away and let me enjoy myself."

He did. Tucker didn't know what foodstuffs Mark kept in the cottage, but there wouldn't be anything fresh. He selected some fruit and a long stick of salami. He decided to skip the beer and got milk instead. And a big box of cornflakes. He liked cornflakes—they comforted him and reminded him of his childhood. With a dozen eggs and a loaf of bread he figured they could make do until he got word to Peterson to send some money.

There wasn't anyone in the store this late except the clerk, but Tucker didn't want to use the public phone. There was no telephone at Mark's, but in the morning he would go over to Cappy's and use his. Cappy could be trusted.

Tucker carried his other selections to the counter where Maggie was waiting, clutching a bottle of shampoo.

"If you can't afford this then put back some of the food," she said with a formidable scowl. "I'd rather go hungry than go one more day without washing my hair."

Tucker raised a brow at that astonishing news. "Right. Die of starvation but make a good-looking corpse. Is that the plan?"

"Whatever you want to call it. I'm getting this shampoo." She hugged the bottle to her breast.

Tucker had no intention of denying the poor girl her shampoo. "What kind of heartless cad do you think I am, anyway?"

"I don't know. How many kinds are there?"

The clerk waited patiently during this exchange, his curiosity barely concealed. Tucker snatched the bottle out of Maggie's hands and thumped it on the counter. "Ring it up," he instructed.

Later they trudged down the road in silence, Tucker hefting the sack of supplies, Maggie fuming beside him. Apparently she hadn't seen the humor in his remark that not only would she get dinner out of the deal but a new purse as well.

Maggie limped along in the misbegotten sneakers, sure that her feet would be irreparably damaged from her ordeal, and sulked. That was something else new, she noted. Normally, she wasn't the sulky type, but Tucker seemed to bring out all her latent personality flaws. Maybe he had been right when he said she needed someone to bring her out of herself. She had felt more emotional ups and downs in the past two days than in her entire life.

But was that good? Wasn't it safer to keep her feelings insulated and protected? Tucker had a native ability to bare all her nerves and leave them exposed, so what would life with him be like? Maggie shoved the notion aside. This was no time to be thinking about the future.

She would be on her own thinking about that; Clementine Kent never got seriously involved with any of her male partners. Maggie realized suddenly that she hadn't had to depend so much on her fictional heroine lately. Maybe she was becoming a more capable person, taking charge of her life. Still, it was getting harder and harder to imagine that life without Tucker in it. And that had Maggie worried.

When at last she spoke it was a murmured "Thanks."

"For what?"

"The shampoo."

Damn, Tucker muttered silently. It didn't seem right for Maggie to be so grateful over such a small thing. It wrenched his heart. "For cripes' sake, Maggie, did you think I wasn't into personal hygiene? I planned to let you buy shampoo."

"I know. I guess I'm just tired and irritable. I've been through a lot in the past forty-eight hours. I used to think it would be exciting to have some adventure in my life. I had no idea it could be so strenuous. I lead a very quiet life, ordinarily," she reminded him.

Tucker looked at her face, which he could barely see in the darkness. He noted the fatigue etched there and he was impressed all over again by her spunk. By her ability to accept a situation most women would have found impossible. "No kidding."

"Really. Why, right now I'd be home in Sallyville, doing my nails and watching TV. The most crucial decision I would have to make would be which outfit to wear tomorrow."

"Yeah, it must be hard to choose between all those chic, glamorous sweaters."

"Why does everyone like to bad-mouth my sweaters?"

Tucker grinned. "You have to admit they're a little on the baggy side. For the first two weeks I thought you were trying to hide something under them. Like your pet Pekingese."

"There isn't a lot to do in Ekalaka in the winter, so I learned to knit at an early age. I started out making sweaters for my brothers and found I liked the loose easy fit." Maggie was struck by something Tucker had said. "Wait a minute. Back up. What did you just say?"

"About your Pekingese?"

"Before that. You said 'for the first two weeks.' What exactly did you mean by that?"

So she hadn't suspected that he'd been following her. At least he had done *something* right. "I've had you under surveillance."

"Surveillance? As in being followed? Watched?"

"That's the only kind of surveillance I studied in G-man school."

Maggie couldn't believe it. But when she thought about it, it all made sense. It explained why Tucker's green sedan had looked so familiar. Why he had been so handy to rescue her from the warehouse. And to think, she had even dismissed the notion of being tailed as patently ridiculous.

She didn't know why it should bother her so much, but it was unnerving that Tucker knew a lot more about her than she did about him. He had invaded her privacy as part of his job. That's what he did for a living. The reality of her situation slammed her right in the heart.

She was a fool for having lulled herself into believing that Tucker was with her because he wanted to be, that everything he did for her was because he cared. In her naiveté, she had pretended that the whole adventure was some romantic escapade and that she had become more to J. P. Tucker than just another assignment.

It was painful to think otherwise.

"So now what's wrong?" he asked in exasperation.

"Nothing."

"Don't give me that. What is it?"

Maggie lengthened her steps and strode away from him. She didn't want him to see the blasted tears that threatened to erupt at any moment. She'd cried more since she'd met him than she had in the past fifteen years combined.

But then, she'd had more to cry about.

"Maggie! Wait! Come back."

She stopped a few yards beyond him and slowly turned around, her heart racing. He was standing in the middle of the dark road. Should she go to him or wait for him to come to her? She didn't want animosity between them, not only because he was her only companion and protector in all this, but because she cared what he thought of her.

"Yes, Tucker," she called softly, invitingly. "What is it?"

"You just passed Mark's cottage. This is it." He jerked a thumb toward a large structure on stilts set back from the road.

She'd have to go to him. She retraced her steps, marched right past him and up the narrow walk made of crushed seashells. She was waiting at the door when he arrived.

Tucker handed Maggie the bag of groceries and jimmied the door of the wide, screened-in porch like an experienced burglar. The latch popped up and he swung it open. "After you, my dear," he said with exaggerated chivalry.

"Why thank you, my *dear*." She couldn't have put less warmth in the word. "What are you waiting for? Get out the key."

"Key? I don't have a key."

"But you said the welcome mat was always out for you here."

"It is, see?" He nudged the large green square of plastic turf with the toe of his loafer. "I just don't happen to have a key. But have no fear, mere locked doors have never deterred J. P. Tucker."

Did locked hearts stand a chance against him? she wondered. "So we add breaking and entering to our list of crimes? You know, Tucker, you've been a bad influence on me. Since I've met you I've been involved in speeding, reckless driving, public drunkenness, aiding and abetting a moonshiner, possible assault and battery and plotting a murder."

He couldn't argue with most of them. "Plotting a murder?"

"Yes. I'm planning to kill you right now."

"Don't forget littering. That one you did all on your own." He shot her a grin guaranteed to melt an ice sculpture, but she only glared at him and hugged the grocery bag tighter.

"I'm waiting. Do you use a credit card, or are you into plastic explosives this year?"

"If I had a credit card we wouldn't be eating salami and cornflakes for dinner. And I'm fresh out of explosives. I'll just have to resort to an old-fashioned but highly efficient means of gaining illegal entry."

"Which is?" she asked with bored disinterest. Before she could draw another breath he had taken the sack from her, whipped her sweater over her head, balled it around one fist and punched out a glass pane in the door. He reached through the new opening, unlocked the door and shrugged modestly. "Works every time."

"I'm sure your friend Mark will appreciate the damage," she said caustically.

"My friend Mark will understand."

The house was damp and smelled of the sea. Maggie ran one hand along the wall to locate a light switch, but when she found it, nothing happened.

"The generator's been shut down for the winter. I can get it started tomorrow when there's light, but I don't want to mess with it tonight," Tucker told her.

"So we sit around in the dark?" she asked peevishly.

"There are a lot of interesting things to do in the dark, but sitting around isn't one of them," Tucker philosophized. "I thought you were tired. Darkness should be no liability for sleeping."

He moved with sureness into the kitchen and opened drawers until he found what he was looking for. He struck a match and lit several candles, placing them in little tin holders. He carried two into the living room and set them on a table. The flickering candlelight threw dancing shadows on the walls but shed enough light to keep them from tripping over each other in the gloom.

"These won't last long, so what do you say we eat and get ready for bed?" At Maggie's nervous jump, Tucker added, "There are two bedrooms, you can have one all to yourself."

She didn't want a bed all to herself. She'd been sleeping alone all her life and now she was getting used to sharing Tucker's warmth. "Fine. That suits me just fine. Is there any hot water for a bath?"

"There will be after I light the water heater. I'll do that now and by the time we're through eating you can have a nice long soak."

They ate in silence, and Maggie wondered at her sudden lack of appetite. It had been days since she'd had a real meal, but even the can of chicken soup she'd found in the cupboard couldn't entice her. She couldn't stop dwelling on the fact that she and Tucker were all alone in this house. They weren't in a motel room and she wasn't handcuffed to the bed. They weren't in a car or the back of a moonshiner's truck, and they weren't out in the open under a canopy of stars.

They were alone in the forced intimacy of a house with real walls and they could do whatever they wanted and not have to worry about being caught at it. It was a heady feeling.

But what did she really want? She had a couple of ideas, even though her experience with men was limited. She'd always read a lot, and not just mysteries, either. There were plenty of steamy romances on her reading list, as well. She knew the "what." It was the "how" that had her so confused.

Tucker munched his salami and tried not to let his glance linger too long on Maggie. How did she manage to look so totally feminine and beautiful after forty-eight hours on the run? No makeup, not so much as a comb, and she looked great. Her blond curls were a wild tangle and she had grimy smudges on her face, but there was something elementally appealing about her unkempt state. It made her look even more vulnerable than she was.

Tucker longed to dampen his finger and rub the dirt away; if he did, maybe he could rub away his driving need for her. But he knew that if he touched her, even if it was only a fingertip to her cheek, he would be lost. He would then have to resort to the action her T-shirt had been taunting him to take.

He was able to resist the temptation only because he knew Maggie Ryan was not ready for anything physical. "Well," he said, breaking the tense silence. "I guess that water's hot by now. I'll run a tub for you."

Maggie stood and gathered their dishes, placing them in the sink. "Don't bother. I can do it myself." She took one of the candles and left, looking, to Tucker's mind, like a wandering waif in a haunted house.

The sound of water splashing into the tub prompted images of Maggie undressing and slipping into it. Those images prompted stirrings in places it wouldn't do Tucker a damned bit of good to have stirrings in. He had to do something.

He knocked lightly on the bathroom door and the soft splashing sound ceased. "Maggie? I just remembered you don't have any fresh clothes, so I rummaged around until I found you some. I'll leave them right outside the door." He knelt and placed the little bundle on the floor. "I think I'll go for a walk along the beach. Put out the candles before you turn in."

"Thank you, Tucker," she said softly.

"Good night, Maggie."

"Good night, Tucker."

Later, when Maggie slipped into the soft cotton nightshirt, she was grateful that Mrs. Mark was her size. She carried her candle into her assigned room and set it on the bedside table. She couldn't see much in the shadowy room, but there would be time tomorrow for exploring her temporary home. Tonight she needed to rest. And in order to do that she would first have to get all thoughts of Tucker out of her mind.

She smiled when she noticed that he had turned back her sheets to air them out and rid them of the pervasive dampness. She climbed into the bed and pulled the crisp percale covers up to her chin, listening to the tide lapping the sand just beyond her window. Here she was, only a few feet from the sea, and still she hadn't seen it.

Probably hadn't occurred to Tucker to wait to let her accompany him on his stroll along the beach. Or if it had, he'd dismissed the idea. Apparently he didn't want to be with her. The thought caused her stomach to tighten into an uncomfortable knot. What would she do if Tucker never returned any of the dizzying feelings that had threatened to overwhelm her during the past two days?

She had not had much time to think the situation through. It seemed they were always on the move, always on the alert for whoever was after them. She still didn't understand how she had gotten so involved in this intrigue; it was too fantastic to be real. She didn't know who those kidnappers were or why she needed Tucker's protection. But she was glad she did.

Was this how love happened? she wondered. Did it just sneak up on a person and clobber them? Maybe this was how Fate worked. Three days ago she didn't even know J. P. Tucker existed, and now . . . now?

Now she wasn't sure what she would do if he went his own way once this was over and they had returned to Washington. Why did the first time she fell in love have to be so complicated? Why did the first guy she ever felt strongly about have to be such an exasperatingly bullheaded, intensely masculine man? Why couldn't she have started out with a safe, nonthreatening shoe salesman or something? And worked her way up to someone as dangerous as Tucker after she'd gained some experience? Clearly she was out of her element and had no idea what to do next.

Maggie wondered if he was attracted to her, if there was any chance that Tucker would ever seriously consider her as a candidate for his affections. She felt more like fifteen than twenty-five, and wished she had paid more attention to Holly's discussions of male-female rituals. If she'd had an iota of Holly's savvy and nerve she wouldn't be lying here alone in a cold bed cringing in doubt and indecision.

No wonder Tucker felt the need to get away from her for a while. He was only doing his job when he took care of her. Now that she was safe he needed his distance.

Maggie hated herself for crying into her pillow like a lovestruck teenager. She hated herself for being immobilized by lack of confidence. She hugged her pillow and wished it were Tucker's hard, warm body in her arms.

She blew out the candle and closed her eyes tightly, conjuring up images of curling against him on a bed of leaves, of being stroked and caressed by his knowing hands, of being kissed by his demanding mouth. Surely the kisses had meant something to him. Surely *she* meant something to him.

Or was he the type to encourage *any* available female? Maggie really knew nothing about men in general, and certainly not this one in particular.

She fell asleep with the sound of the sea in her ears, and thoughts of Tucker in her mind.

The wind from the Atlantic was cool, and Tucker tugged his jacket closer. When he started out he'd had no real plan in mind; he only knew he did not want to be in the house when Maggie stepped, fresh and flushed, from her bath. He'd spent years cultivating self-control and discipline, but he couldn't seem to think beyond the moment where she was concerned.

It would be foolish, if not fatal, to start anything with a woman like Maggie. He was relatively certain that she had never been with a man, and he had no intentions of seducing a virgin—despite the fact that he'd had a hard time remembering that in the back of Pirdy Lee's truck.

That had happened to his mother thirty-five years ago, and he was the result. He would never risk making that mistake. He would never put Maggie through the kind of hell his own mother had been through. Of course, times had changed. Single mothers were more prevalent today, but that did not make their lot any easier. Besides, he told himself with a sharp shake of his head, when and *if* he ever decided to start a family, it would be with the benefit of marriage. And the woman would be ready to make the commitment, ready and willing to take the fatal step.

He refused to get caught up in a heated moment that could irrevocably change both their lives forever. He also did not want to be forced into a marriage against his will, for the thought of abandoning a woman in trouble would simply never occur to him. Tucker wasn't in favor of lavish weddings, but he sure didn't want to have it catered by Smith and Wesson.

Marriage! Why was that thought on his mind? Because, he answered himself, Maggie was that kind of woman. And all the more reason to keep her inviolate.

Thinking about her was doing nothing for his peace of mind, so Tucker tried to force his thoughts to take a different tack.

There were things he needed to sort through, things he needed to figure out. Tomorrow he would go to Cappy's and call Baker. Maybe his partner had some news, or a few clues as to how those crooks had tracked them so far. Maybe the department had picked them up by now and he would get the all clear to return to D.C. That would be a relief.

Or would it? What would become of his and Maggie's relationship when they got out of this mess? Relationship?

Who was he kidding? The only thing they had was a forced togetherness.

Maggie was a frightened young woman caught in a swirl of uncertainty, and she was clinging to the only life support available. Him. Didn't hostages sometimes even fall for their captors?

Tucker had come to mean safety to her and that was all. It would pay him to keep that in mind for as long as they were forced to remain together in such intimate isolation. In fact, it would pay him to discourage her as much as possible.

Why did he have to care about her feelings so much? He wished he could just take what she was unknowingly offering and let it go at that. But for the first time in his life he thought of a woman as a person with real feelings, a complex being who was more than just a warm body. What made the whole thing so damned laughable was that she wasn't his type at all. If he hadn't been assigned the duty of following her around, he never would have noticed her.

Well, he admitted grudgingly, he would have *noticed* her. Legs like hers would have gotten his attention eventually. But he and Maggie Ryan had nothing in common. They did not have the same values and they came from entirely different worlds.

They had no future.

Tucker stood on the beach for a long time, watching wave after wave race to the shore, the moonlight slapping and dancing on the surface of the tumbling water. He looked far out to the horizon where the blackness of the ocean blended with the blackness of the night sky. He breathed deeply of the sea-salt smell and tried to dispel all thoughts of the soft blond woman who lay sleeping peacefully in the house on the other side of the dunes. He tried to deny the ache of desire that such thoughts provoked.

He tried, in vain, to imagine a future without Maggie Ryan.

Chapter Eight

Maggie awoke early as was her custom and dressed in the clothes Tucker had provided. She slipped the white tank top on first, then put a green cotton shirt over it and knotted it at her waist. The white duck drawstring pants were too short for her long legs, so she rolled them up into a cuff at mid-calf.

Brushing out her hair in the mirror over the dresser, she decided she would pass. She longed for some makeup to hide the ravages of her tearful night, but since none was available she pinched her cheeks and hoped the sea air would put some color into her face.

Maggie listened quietly outside Tucker's door but there were no sounds indicating he was up. She wandered around the house, familiarizing herself with the small bungalow. Besides the two bedrooms and bath, there was a large airy kitchen with windows on two walls. This adjoined a long combination dining-living room, and the whole was furnished with old but serviceable pieces.

There were books on low shelves under the window in the living room and an assortment of board games on a table in the corner. The wood floor was bare, and Maggie decided it was probably too much trouble to be continually shaking sand out of rugs. All in all, it was quite pleasant, a fine place to be holed up in for the duration.

In the kitchen she found a box of tea bags and set a kettle on to boil. When her tea was ready she carried it out to the big screened-in porch, where she got her first glimpse of the ocean. Just beyond the dunes, it shimmered like gray-green glass in the bright morning sun. There had once been a fence between the house and the beach, but all that was left of it were a few lone posts tilting among the abundant crop of sea grass. Atop one of the weathered posts a large seabird flapped and squawked.

Its voice blended with those of the swooping gulls, and Maggie watched in fascinated wonder as they dive-bombed into the water and came up a second later with breakfast. She was torn between the desire to wiggle her bare feet in the sand and the need to wait for Tucker to awake and go with her. She wanted the two memories to be inexorably woven in her mind—her first experience with sun-warmed sand between her toes and Tucker's fingers tangled with hers. She could wait.

She drank two more cups of tea and between each listened outside his door for sounds of life. How could anyone sleep so late? she wondered. Early rising, like well-cared-for teeth, had been considered a virtue in her family, and she'd always felt that morning was the best part of the day.

She glanced at her watch. It was nearly nine o'clock. She'd give him another half hour to laze away and then she was going to demand that he get up and keep her company.

A groggy Tucker peered out the door a few minutes later. "You up already?" he asked in a raspy morning voice.

Maggie's heart thudded at the sight of him. His eyes were heavy-lidded with sleep and his cheeks dark with stubble. He hadn't bothered to comb his hair and it was mussed from tossing and turning. He had on an unfamiliar pair of navy blue shorts and held a nautical-looking T-shirt that she watched him pull over his bare chest. Again she noticed how well muscled his legs were and how they were covered with golden brown hair.

Maggie hadn't realized she was holding her breath until she spoke and it came out in a rush. "Yes. I've been up for a couple of hours. The early bird catches the worm, you know."

"So I've heard," he mumbled as he turned toward the kitchen and the added incentive of a few dozen cups of black coffee. "But who wants worms for breakfast?"

Maggie followed him. "I'd be glad to fix you something. We don't have any grits and I don't know how to make biscuits, but I saw some maple syrup in the cupboard. Would you like some French toast?" she asked cheerfully.

Tucker shuddered. "French toast? In the morning?" He found the jar of instant coffee and dumped a hearty load into a big mug, then filled it with hot water from the kettle. "I don't think so, Maggie. Thanks just the same. Cornflakes will be fine." He headed for the refrigerator but she beat him there.

"Let me fix them for you. You take your coffee out to the porch and I'll bring you a nice bowl of cereal. How about some plain toast to go with it?" She wanted to prepare his food. It seemed a very intimate thing to do.

Tucker peered at her beaming face through bleary eyes. She was probably one of those women who really got excited in the kitchen. One who liked doing things domestic and had "homemaker" encoded in her DNA. So be it. Who was he to deny her the pleasure of waiting on him? "Sure, plain toast would be fine."

He hated mornings, anyhow, and tolerated them because it was the only known way to get to afternoon. He took a big gulp of the hot coffee and padded out to the porch, where it took several moments for his eyes to adjust to the blinding sunlight.

"So what do you want to do today?" Maggie asked brightly as she stacked the dishes in the sink. Tucker hadn't said a half dozen words all through breakfast, but maybe if she asked him a direct question he would feel obligated, by good breeding, to answer.

"Do?"

"Yes, do. We don't have to hide out here in this house, do we? Wouldn't it be safe to get out and explore some?"

"Maggie, I've been down here dozens of times and there isn't that much to do. It's too cold to swim, but if you want to work on your tan you won't find much competition for sand space."

She pouted, and Tucker wondered if she was conscious of how pretty she looked doing it. "Well," she said as she squirted detergent into the sink. "I just thought it might be fun if you showed me around. I've never even seen the ocean before, and this is new and exciting to me."

He relented at the real disappointment in her face. "You've never seen the ocean?"

"I'm from Montana," she reminded him dryly.

"Oh, yeah. We could walk over to Cappy's later. I want to let him know we're here and I think I'll call Baker and see what's gone down since we left D.C."

"Who's Cappy?"

"A great old guy who's lived here all his life. He has a fishing boat, and during the summer season he makes a good living hauling tourists out to the best fishing spots. Wait till you meet him; he makes Popeye look like a landlubber."

Maggie smiled. "He sounds interesting. I can't wait to meet him; can we go soon?"

"Sure," Tucker answered, settling back onto the couch. "As soon as you wash those dishes."

A dish towel sailed the length of the room to land damply on his face. "As soon as *we* wash these dishes, you mean."

Cappy was everything Tucker had said and more. His face was pinched and wizened and a sparse white stubble glared in contrast to his nut-brown skin. His pale gray eyes were set in a perpetual squint from staring out to sea, and a thick shelf of wild, white brows offered little protection from the relentless sun. Maggie scanned her vocabulary for a suitable term to describe the wiry little man. Crusty curmudgeon sprang readily to mind.

Tucker explained their situation as best he could but Cappy held up a restraining hand. "Don't need to tell me more, Tuck, my boy. I got secrets, you got secrets. We all got secrets. If this is some kind of guv'mint business then it ain't no business of mine, so let's just leave it there."

Tucker smiled gratefully. He knew Cappy would understand and not pry. "Thanks, Cappy. I need to use your phone, though. Would that be all right?"

"Sure thing. Why don't I take Maggie here out to the pier and show her the *Thalassa*? When you're done, come on out."

The *Thalassa* turned out to be Cappy's boat, and he was rightfully proud of her. Her hull gleamed and sparkled in the sun, and a pure-white canvas awning snapped in the breeze. It was clear to Maggie, who knew absolutely nothing about boats, who, in fact, had never been in anything larger than a canoe, that the *Thalassa* was a fine, seaworthy vessel. She followed Cappy across the swaying gangplank and stepped aboard.

He showed her below and all around the boat, pointing out things of interest as though she understood all his nautical talk. Maggie nodded appreciatively and when the tour was over they settled down in clean white deck chairs.

"How long you known Tucker?" he asked unexpectedly.

"Ah . . . three days. He's already saved my life twice."

Cappy snorted. "Yep. That's Tucker. He's a dedicated guv'mint man. But not like most of 'em, nosiree. Tucker's smart too. If it ever came to choosin' up sides for any kind of tussle, I'd want J. P. Tucker on my team."

"How long have you known him, Cappy?"

The old man tilted back the disreputable-looking yachtsman's cap he wore and scratched his grizzled head. "That'll be about thirteen years now, I reckon. He first started comin' down here while he was in college. Mark Sumter's folks owned the beach house in them days, and he and Mark were thick as thieves." He chuckled. "I recall, they had their share of wild weekend parties down here. Course, Mr. and Miz Sumter never knew about that."

Maggie tried to imagine a young, carefree Tucker splashing in the surf with a lithe girl in a bikini, drinking beer in the hot sun. She had trouble with the image. "So he's known Mark a long time?"

"Yep. They went into the army after school. I think that was all Mark's idea; he was a gung-ho kind of kid in them days. Too bad about Mark," Cappy said, almost to himself.

"What about him?"

"Didn't Tuck tell you? They just got in on the tail end of the war, but Mark lost an arm overseas and got an early discharge. Tucker stayed until he finished his tour. You know," he said thoughtfully, "now that I reckon on it, it seems that Tuck never was the same after he got back."

Maggie couldn't bear to think of Tucker amid the horrors of war. She grieved silently for the young man he had once been. "What about Mark?"

"Oh, well, he's married now and has three kids. Little Peter is turning out to be quite a fisherman. Mark's got a desk job with the IRS and they all live in some suburb or t'other. He and his family have been coming down here every summer since his folks died and left him the house."

"And does Tucker come down very often?"

Cappy appeared to gather his thoughts. "Nope. Not near as often as I'd like to see him. Then, Tuck's a loner. Always was, even when he was surrounded by folks."

"Cappy? Would you mind answering a question for me?"

"Not if I can."

"What does J.P. stand for? Why does Tucker use only his initials and prefer to be called by his last name?"

This time Cappy scratched his stubby chin. "J.P., huh? Why, I never give it much thought. I allus just thought of him as Tucker. Never knew no different."

Maggie leaned back in the deck chair and let the October sunshine warm her. The more she found out about Tucker, the less she understood. "Thanks, Cappy."

The rest of the afternoon was spent exploring the small settlement. Maggie and Tucker walked up and down the wide, white beach and then made a cursory examination of some of the small shops. Most of them had closed for the season, so they contented themselves with looking in the windows. As Tucker explained, they didn't have any money for shopping, anyway.

But when they stopped at the general store to buy a few necessities, Tucker handed Maggie a folded bill.

"What's this for?" she asked, surprised.

"For whatever you need. I know you probably need some girl stuff." He pushed the money at her. "Go on, take it. We can spare it. Baker's mailing me a cashier's check."

Her face brightened and again it struck Tucker that a woman like Maggie shouldn't have to do without things. He wished he could give her everything she wanted, everything she needed. As it was, a new lipstick was about all he could afford. Not only financially, but emotionally, as well.

The things Maggie Ryan needed were things Tucker had never been able to give to anyone.

"I found some real bargains," she gushed later when she joined him on the store steps. "It's going to feel so good to look like a woman again."

"So what have you been looking like? Chopped liver?"

Maggie frowned. "You know what I mean." She linked her arm in his. "Are you going to tell me what you found out when you talked to your partner?"

"Not much." Tucker wasn't sure he wanted to be so close to her, yet he didn't have the inclination or willpower to move away. "He promised to keep me posted but he doesn't know anything yet. I asked him to keep it under his hat about where we are, not to tell anyone. Not even the department."

"Why? You don't suspect one of your fellow agents is mixed up with those guys at the warehouse, do you?"

"I don't know what to think. When it comes to counterfeiting there are all kinds of motives—especially greed. I just don't want to take any chances." He couldn't add that he didn't want to place her in any more danger.

"I still don't understand what this has to do with me. What was supposed to be in that envelope that Haversham told those thugs he gave me?"

Tucker looked at her, trying to assess her position and his. What should he tell her? How much of the truth? He had long since given up any notion of her involvement, but at times the less a person knew the better off they were. "How about if we just drop the subject for now? Maybe when this mess is straightened out I can fill you in."

"Classified information, huh, G-man?"

"You might say that, Legs."

"Okay," she capitulated. "I'll let you off easily this time since it's too nice a day to think about crime. Just remember that the subject can be reopened at a later date."

"Deal."

They walked down the dusty main street, their clasped hands swinging between them. Unlike the indomitable Clementine, Maggie didn't really want to know all the details. It was enough to know that she was here in this beautiful place with Tucker. It was enough to know that she had him all to herself for an indeterminate amount of time. It was enough to know that he was stuck with her whether he wanted to be or not.

But could that really be enough? an annoying little voice asked her.

"Fleet's in," Tucker said with a smile.

Maggie glanced along his outstretched arm and saw the fishing boats gliding into the pier. "What do you think today's catch is?"

"Beats me. Want to go find out? I'd love some fresh seafood, so long as it doesn't come in a shell."

"Why is that?"

"Allergy," he explained succinctly.

"There go my two favorites, lobster and shrimp. It also eliminates my third choice, oysters. Let's find out what's left."

The fresh bluefish they bought cooked up beautifully and they ate at the picnic table on the porch. The dishes were ignored as they watched the sunset turn the water crimson and gold. They talked softly about nothing of consequence and the night closed in with a seductive intimacy they really didn't need.

"How long do you think we'll have to stay here, Tucker?"

"Until it's safe to go back."

"But will that be days? Or weeks?" Maggie didn't want to go back at all. Being near the sea with Tucker was like a slice of life out of time, out of place. She knew it couldn't last forever, but that didn't stop her from wishing it would.

"I don't know," he said impatiently. "What's your hurry to get back? Leave an anxious lover behind?" The question came out more petulantly than he had planned.

"If you've been doing your job the past two weeks, you should know that isn't the case. I was just curious, that's all."

"I don't know, Maggie. I hope this will be over soon."

"I guess I won't have a job at Haversham Photography when I get back."

"There won't be a Haversham Photography when you get back."

"Right. I'll have to find another job."

"I guess. What do you want to do?"

"Sculpt."

"Sculpt?"

"You know, to model likenesses in clay? You've heard of sculpture before, haven't you?"

"Yes, I've heard of sculpture. It's just that I'd forgotten that you do it. Much money in it?"

"Not so far. But I managed to get a gallery in Georgetown to display some of my work." Her voice took on an excited tone. "The owner was very enthusiastic about it."

"So what do you sculpt?" he asked, hoping she wasn't one of those artists who made big abstract sculptures with holes in the middle and gave them names like *Realities of the Universe*.

"Mostly figures and busts. I like working with people—live models. It adds vitality to the work."

Tucker shifted in his chair. "I guess someone like Cappy would make an interesting subject." He knew nothing about art and wouldn't be able to bluff this topic very far. He'd spent his college days in marketing and finance classes and his nights in stupid, mindless pursuits. He hadn't seen any art galleries in Southeast Asia and so far he'd managed to avoid them in D.C.

"He'd make a great character study. Maybe I'll buy some paper and charcoal and try some sketches of him." She scooted her chair closer to Tucker. "The person I'd really like to model is you."

"Me?" Tucker glanced at Maggie and found her studying him with a very un-Maggie-like intensity.

"You have a firm, bold jawline." She ran her forefinger along it gently and watched a muscle clench. "Your nose is as fine and straight as any on an old Roman coin." Her finger skidded down its length enticingly and Tucker felt his stomach go all woozy. "But the best part of your whole face is your lips." The pad of her finger found the indentation above his upper lip and lingered there before easing around the edges of his mouth with excruciating slowness. "They're soft and full—even when you're angry."

Tucker felt the heat gathering inside him and his mind cast around for something to say that would break the tension. His mind seemed to be on downtime while all other systems were blinking go. He allowed Maggie's finger to slip between his lips and caught it with his teeth, testing its daintiness.

It was the natural thing to do.

He leaned over and eased her onto his lap, finding her weight delightful. Her arms slipped around his neck and he was aware of her fingers twining in his hair, caressing the nape of his neck where it was trimmed short. The only sound he heard was their breathing—and a persistent pounding that was either the surf or the clamor of Tucker's blood.

Single-handedly, he worried the knot at the bottom of Maggie's shirt and was surprised and relieved when she took over the task.

Their gazes locked, and Maggie wondered whether she just might be playing with fire. She was sure of it when his lips lowered to hers and kissed her as she had never before been kissed. There was nothing tentative about the way Tucker's mouth eased hers open. There was nothing restrained about the way his tongue sought and parried the warm shaft of her own. There was nothing reserved about the insistence of his passion as he pressed against her.

This was a Tucker she hadn't seen before, an uncautious, uncontrolled Tucker, whose unbridled passion was evident in his every move. His hand caressed her breast through the thin fabric of her top, and her nipple surged at his touch, eager to yield to his every demand. She moaned in protest when he withdrew, then sighed with pleasure when he slipped beneath the shirt to cup her aching flesh.

"Maggie, Maggie," he breathed. "You've had it."

"Not yet."

"Maggie, you don't know what you're doing to me."

She shifted restlessly on his lap and heard the soft whoosh of his breath as he gasped. "I have a fair idea," she teased.

"God, woman, I'm not made of stone."

She glanced downward slyly, then let her gaze travel provocatively back up to his. "No?"

Tucker tried to think. He tried to summon up the discipline of all his years of survival training, but it had been replaced by a far more primitive set of drives. He scooped her into his arms and stood shakily. Her lips sought and fastened on his while he carried her to the padded glider on the far end of the porch.

He'd never walked so far in his life.

As she was eased down on the cushions, Maggie trailed her arms out of the green overshirt. She stretched out languidly and Tucker sat on the edge of the glider beside her. The night was mysterious with erotic promise, the relentless surf as primitive as a pagan drum.

It seemed to Maggie that the sound matched the tempo of her heart's wild beating. She felt the cool breeze on her heated skin as Tucker slowly drew the cotton top upward.

He replaced it with the warm moistness of his mouth and kissed each centimeter of skin as it was exposed. His hands shaped the mounds of her breasts and he teased and tugged on each aroused bud until Maggie was sure she would die of pleasure. She had never suspected that a man's touch could ignite such fiery responses. She had never guessed that she was capable of such passion.

Tucker's body tensed until he thought he would choke from the effort to control himself. His lips danced over Maggie's silky skin, and every surprised gasp of pleasure he provoked drove him nearer to the brink of insanity. He had never wanted a woman as much as he wanted Maggie Ryan. He had never wanted a woman to want him as much as he hoped she did. He'd always believed in mutual satisfaction, but it suddenly became vital for him to thrust aside his own needs in an effort to fully gratify hers.

"Oh, Tucker," she sighed. Her eyes were closed now, and all her senses focused on the points where his skin touched hers. "I had no idea I could feel this way."

His fires burned hotter at the thought that he was exploring uncharted territory. Maggie's lifelong impressions of lovemaking would be forever colored by what he did or did not do right now. She was a totally clean slate upon which he could record a sensuous saga.

He was a totally daunted coward.

Tucker sat up abruptly and tugged the thin shirt down so far that it stretched at the neckline. He started counting slowly, silently, waiting for his good sense and keen discipline to take over. There was no way he was going to carry this to the ultimate conclusion. He had responsibilities. To Maggie. Both as a tax-paying citizen in need of his protection, and as an uninitiated female. To say nothing of his responsibility to the U.S. government.

He was older and more worldly than she, and it would be unfair for him to take advantage of her even if she *was* the one who had started the whole thing. Somebody had to be strong and it had damned well better be him.

Maggie blinked in disbelief. The warmth and power had been rudely switched off, and she felt as if she had just been snatched from a particularly pleasant dream.

"What's wrong?" she asked in a quiet voice.

"Nothing." Tucker had to put distance between her trembling body and his own aching one. He leaped to his feet and paced to the door of the porch. He stood and stared out over the dunes to the endless expanse of ocean, methodically matching the twinkling reflections of the stars with their celestial sources. He wished he was back protecting aging presidential widows.

As long as he and Maggie were together, he was destined to spend an inordinate amount of time looking out to sea. He knew he couldn't bear to see the disappointment on her face.

"Well, if nothing is wrong, will you kindly tell me what happened? One minute you're kissing my breasts and the next minute you're not. Did you encounter something unpleasant?"

Tucker winced at her honest summary of his actions. "Of course I didn't encounter anything unpleasant. How could you even think such a thing?" He continued to stare out to sea.

"Weren't you enjoying it at all?" she asked innocently.

"Yes, dammit! I was enjoying it too much."

"Then what? If you're giving up fulfillment for Lent, you're a few months premature." Maggie blinked back the brimming tears and swallowed convulsively in an effort to keep them out of her voice. She was hurt and angry—the conditions most likely to prompt an embarrassing crying jag. Anger inched out the hurt, which she hoped to hide from him.

"Maggie. Just go inside and go to bed."

"With you?"

"No! Not with me."

She folded her arms over her breasts. "Turn around and look at me, J. P. Tucker," she demanded in a voice like quiet thunder.

"I'd rather not, if you don't mind."

"I *do* mind." She stood and grabbed him by the shoulders and spun him around before he knew what was happening.

She glared at him and he glared back at her. "I'd just as soon drop the subject for tonight, Maggie," he muttered through clenched teeth.

"I'd just as soon discuss it," she retorted.

"All right." He folded his arms in an imitation of her own body language. "To save time on this discussion, I'd like to say up front that I have no intention of making love to you, Maggie Ryan."

"Is that so?"

"Yes."

"Could have fooled me!" she said with a derisive snort.

"Anyone could fool you, Maggie. You're a baby."

"A baby?"

"That's right."

"I'm twenty-five years old."

"You may be twenty-five chronologically, but with your inexperience you're about fifteen emotionally."

"That makes me—what?—175 in doggie years. Is that old enough for you?"

Tucker's eyes widened in exasperation. Why did she have to be so damned cute? If he wasn't careful she was going to start him laughing and that would be the beginning of the end. "It's not a question of age."

"So what's it a question of?"

"I'm not going to be the one," he blurted out.

"The 'one'? The one to what? Relieve me of my virtue? What's the matter? Are you afraid I'll scream for reinforcements? That my father and four vicious brothers will come on a cavalry charge all the way from Montana?"

"I'm not afraid of anything."

"Oh, yes you are, Tucker," she pronounced with triumph. "You are afraid of me."

"That's ridiculous."

"Is it?"

"Dammit. This is neither the time nor the place for...well...for what might have happened here tonight." It suddenly struck him that he was defending himself for having noble intentions. What had happened to the world?

"So why did you get me started?" she demanded.

"Get *you* started?" he asked incredulously. "What about all that 'you have such a firm jawline' crap? I'd say you were jump-started before you even sucked me in with that stuff."

"Sucked you in?" Now it was Maggie's turn to sound insulted. "You seemed perfectly willing to me."

God! How did she do this to him?

Tucker stared at her, wide-eyed, unable to think of a suitable rebuke.

"You know what your problem is, J. P. Tucker?"

"No, but will it take long for you to tell me?" he asked resignedly.

"Not very. Your problem is that you're a tease."

"What?" he shrieked in a very unmacho way.

"A tease," she repeated through gritted teeth. "You got me all worked up, all ready to go for the biggie, and then you just turned it off. Well, maybe you can do that with your feelings. Or maybe you don't even have any—I'm not sure yet. But I can't. What do you think? That I have ice water in my veins?"

It occurred to Tucker that it was unfortunate he didn't have a tape recorder with him. Nobody would ever believe this conversation. He'd just used every ounce of control he possessed, every resource known to modern man, to avoid taking the woman's virginity, and she was calling *him* a tease.

He tipped back his head and laughed.

"What the hell are you laughing at?" she demanded.

"You. Really, Maggie, you are too much."

She failed to see any humor in the situation and barely suppressed the urge to stamp her foot like the heroine in some period novel. Better yet, she wanted to grab him by the shirtfront and shake him until his empty head rattled. She wanted to kick his shins and scratch his face. How dare he laugh at her! How dare he?

Most of all she wanted him to grab her and kiss her again. She wanted to be reassured that it hadn't all been an illusion, a perfect dream that had come from her imagination.

"I hate you, and you can take your honor and . . ." She decided not to tell him where to stuff it. He could figure it out for himself. Maggie spun on her heel and stormed away from him.

He followed her, still laughing. "You don't hate me," he cajoled.

She stood in the doorway to her room, and Tucker thought he'd never seen a woman more vital or more in need of ravishing.

"The hell I don't," she answered back, slamming the door in his face.

He went into his own room and closed the door quietly. No satisfaction there.

He opened it and slammed it with a resounding bang that was probably heard all the way to Kill Devil Hills.

Chapter Nine

During the days that followed, Tucker and Maggie managed to avoid situations that might lead to a replay of the scene on the veranda. Through concentrated effort they were able to live together in the close confines of the house by the sea and yet shun any real intimacy. They soon settled into a routine and divided the tasks of daily living equally.

Maggie rose early and drank her tea before taking her new sketchbook and charcoal pencils out to the beach for a couple of hours of sketching. She drew endless pictures of water birds, fishing boats and the waves crashing against the pier.

She trekked over to Cappy's and sketched the old man as he went about his business. Her sketchbook filled rapidly and she decided she would have ample material once she returned home. Cappy took her out fishing with him and, as much as she enjoyed her new freedom, Maggie found herself anxious to return to Tucker.

Sometimes, when she settled down to draw a diving gull, she was surprised when the stroke that was supposed to be a sweeping wing turned into the planes of a ruggedly handsome face. She could draw Tucker from memory, so permanently stamped on her consciousness was his image. She captured all his moods, the lopsided grin he flashed when he was amused, the thunderous scowl that darkened his face when he was not, the pensive concentration when he didn't know she was watching him. She never let him see the sketches because she did not want him to know how fully he occupied her thoughts.

Maggie made her tea and glanced out the kitchen window. There would be no escape today. The sky was dark and forbidding, the waves scudding before a strong wind that pelted the beach house with rain. She sat at the table, trying to write another letter to her parents, but what she intended to be reassurance that she was well and happy was turning into a detailed list extolling Tucker's virtues. She crumpled the paper and tossed it aside.

She couldn't reveal her situation to her family just yet. She gave up on letter writing and, as always when her mind was idle, her thoughts turned to Tucker.

Deep in her heart, in the place where she kept feelings too fragile to examine in the light of day, Maggie knew that her future was inexorably tangled with that of J. P. Tucker. Unfortunately, he was determined not to allow her into his life, and she didn't have the resources to fight his stubborn indifference.

He seemed barely able to tolerate being in the same room with her, and he frequently jumped up after dinner to announce that he was going out. Alone. Maggie had no idea where he went on these nighttime excursions, but it seemed obvious that he didn't care to spend any more time with her than was absolutely necessary.

The days weren't so bad. They rented bikes in the village one day and rode over to the Fort Raleigh National Historical Site to poke around, and discovered they shared an interest in history. They packed a lunch and pedaled into Kitty Hawk for a look at the Wright Brothers Memorial, then ventured as far as their legs would take them along the Cape Hatteras National Seashore.

Sometimes it seemed to Maggie that Tucker was bent on bringing about their total physical exhaustion with so much roadwork. It certainly wasn't the kind of workout she had envisioned the night she tempted him onto the glider.

But the man could be a rock when he wanted to be, and lately he'd been as stony as Mount Rushmore. On occasion, Maggie tried to tease him into a more pleasant mood, but he was about as jolly as a wet cat. She cursed her inexperience and wondered if things would be different were she not burdened with virginity.

It really was funny. She'd always assumed that the man she loved would be glad she had saved herself for him. She'd never considered virtue such a liability before.

But it was. Sometimes Maggie would look up and find Tucker watching her intently. Then he would glance away quickly and pretend interest in something else. Their conversations around the house took on a stilted formality, and Maggie soon understood what was happening. Tucker was putting as much distance as possible between them. She felt a sense of loss for all they'd shared but could never have again. Why did he have to be such a fool?

Tucker lay in bed and listened to the storm lashing the little house. He checked his watch and was surprised at the late hour—it was still quite dark. He wondered how much longer he could hide out in his room before Maggie came tapping to roust him. Maggie with her effervescent smile and ready humor. Maggie, whose green eyes lowered with hurt whenever he left her alone.

But dammit! A man had his limits. He couldn't be expected to spend day after day in such close proximity without once losing his control, could he? Yes, he answered himself. He was expected to do just that, because if he slipped so much as an inch, if they exchanged so much as a handshake, he might as well kiss his good intentions goodbye.

Tucker was made of stern stuff, but the effort required to tamp down his desire, to quell his need to touch her, to choke back the words that threatened every time he opened his mouth, was beginning to try his patience. He had thought to work it off with physical activity, but that only made him want to collapse into bed. But every time he got near the bed he thought about how wonderful it would be to have Maggie there beside him, and the vicious cycle would start all over again.

He would have to get up soon and face her, but the day loomed ahead like Chinese water torture. If they spent the day closed up in the house, his self-control would be chipped away bit by bit. Every time she smiled. Every time she looked up at him through lowered lashes. Every time she moved, barefoot, across the room. God, he's sworn service to his country, but this was asking too much.

He yanked the covers over his head and tossed them to one side. He could hear her out there, running water into the kettle, opening a window. He pictured her standing before it, breathing deeply. He imagined her breasts lifting with each breath, her eyes closed to fully savor the scent of the rain. Without conscious effort he saw himself walking silently up behind her, wrapping his arms around her waist, drawing her back against him. He could smell the freshness of her hair and knew all too well how it would feel to bury his face in the shiny cascade of curls....

Dammit! He tossed to the other side. This was getting him nowhere. His time would be better spent puzzling out the case. He'd talked to his partner the night before, and John had informed him that so far the counterfeiters had evaded capture.

Haversham had been no help; he claimed not to know who "the boss" was. It was apparent that whoever he was, he was the brains behind the operation. Those guys at the warehouse hadn't displayed the intelligence to plan and execute such a scheme and were probably just hired muscle.

The designs for the bills were still missing, and Haversham maintained he had given them to Maggie. However, he had finally admitted that she was not in on the deal and had not been aware of the transaction. He'd slipped them into her bag right before sending her home for the day.

But those thugs at the warehouse had searched Maggie's purse and apartment and the designs had not been found. Was it possible that she *did* have them? If she wasn't involved, she couldn't have passed them to anyone else. Was it possible that she had discovered the plans and decided to go into business for herself? Tucker tried to separate his personal feelings for Maggie from his professional instincts, but it didn't add up.

Still, Maggie was the only lead he had, and Tucker knew he would have to confront her soon. Soon, like today.

Maggie was curled up on the sofa with a paperback novel when Tucker emerged from his room some time later.

"Good morning." She looked up and smiled. "I was getting worried about you."

"Why?"

"Well, you don't usually sleep so late."

"I wasn't sleeping," he confessed as he made a cup of instant coffee.

"Oh." That meant he was avoiding her. That's what he didn't say, but what she knew was true, anyway.

He brought his coffee into the living room and sat in a chair opposite her. "Quite a storm."

"Yes, it is." They might as well have been strangers on a bus.

"Maggie..." Tucker hesitated to broach the subject he had been giving so much thought to. But he had to do it.

"Yes?"

"We need to talk."

She sighed with relief. Finally. It was about time they started talking and stopped pussyfooting around each other like a couple of wary opponents. "Yes, we do."

"I want you to tell me everything that happened the day you were abducted. Start with getting up and don't leave anything out. Who did you see, who did you speak to? Even on the phone. It's important to the case, Maggie, that you remember everything."

So it was the case he wished to discuss. She might have known. Always the case, his duty. He couldn't be a man in love. No, he would always be a Secret Service agent first. Maggie felt defeated and sad, but she spent a few minutes gathering her thoughts.

If Tucker said something was important, it was, and she would do her best to give him an accurate picture of all that had happened to her that day. It didn't matter that the only event worth mentioning was her meeting with J. P. Tucker.

She outlined her every move. Because she was such a creature of habit, it was not difficult for her to recall events that had occurred nearly two weeks before. When she got to the part about the teenager stealing her tote bag, Tucker sat forward excitedly.

"What was in the bag, Maggie?" Maybe Haversham had planted the designs in the tote, and not her purse.

"Nothing, really. I had taken the book I was reading out of it. I used the bag to carry a pair of loafers that morning, but I dropped them off at the repair shop on my lunch hour."

"So it was empty?"

"Yes, I guess so. It was an old bag, not at all valuable. I can't imagine why anyone would want to steal it."

"Neither can I," Tucker muttered. Was it possible that yet a third faction could be involved? "Describe the guy on the bus as carefully as you can," he commanded.

"He was just a kid. Fourteen or fifteen. Sandy-colored hair, grubby clothes. I remember thinking that he must not have been a very accomplished purse snatcher."

"And did you report the theft?"

"Report it? You mean to the police?" At his nod she went on. "Of course not. There wasn't anything of value stolen."

Just plans for a hundred-dollar bill so perfect that it could fool an expert. Tucker collapsed back on the sofa cushions and massaged his temples. He hoped to hell that kid didn't have serious crime connections, or a part-time job as an engraver.

But, no, he decided, only an accomplished counterfeiter would recognize the value of the plans, and it would take someone with Haversham's skill to execute the plates competently.

To a young street kid, the envelope probably appeared worthless, and with any luck it had been trashed with the worn-out tote bag. By now, the elusive plans that everyone, good guys and bad guys alike, were scrambling for were probably no more than ashes floating in the air over the Sallyville Municipal Dump.

"What is it, Tucker? What's that silly grin for?"

He told her.

"You mean I really did have the envelope the weasel was after?"

"Temporarily."

Maggie considered this. "What would have happened to me if that kid hadn't swiped my bag? What would those guys have done if they'd found the plans in my apartment?" She shuddered and braced herself for Tucker's answer.

"Probably nothing," he lied. No point scaring her now that the worst was over. "They'd have left with the envelope and you would have been none the wiser."

"But I still don't understand. How does Mr. Haversham figure in all of this?"

Tucker related what John Baker had told him. "Haversham is an ex-con who just happens to be a master engraver. He was serving a sentence on another counterfeiting charge at the same time as Jiggs Skirby."

"Skirby? Sounds like something you should get a shot for. Who is he?"

"Another ex-con with a long history of counterfeiting arrests. The last one was just a few years go. He's violating his parole somewhere in Mexico at the moment."

"Mexico?" Maggie's eyes brightened. "Mr. Haversham went to Mexico a few weeks ago. He said it was business."

"Yeah, bad business. That's the connection we've been looking for. Haversham must have smuggled the plans back into the country."

"But how did Skirby get them to Mexico in the first place?"

"That's a good question. He didn't design them himself, so he must have a connection with someone at the Bureau of Engraving."

"You mean someone with the government is involved?"

"The way the system is set up, only an insider could have the knowledge to create such a perfect bogus bill. Even then it would be hard, since the engravers all work on different parts of the plates and no one is supposed to see the whole thing."

"I still don't understand why Mr. Haversham slipped the envelope into my bag."

"Evidently he got nervous." Tucker had an idea. "Did anyone come into the studio that day, anyone I missed in my surveillance? Someone you didn't recognize as a customer?"

Maggie reached back into her memory for any detail that might help Tucker. "You know, there was a man. He must have used the alley entrance, because I didn't see him come in. I didn't even know anyone was in the studio until I heard angry voices. I was concerned about Mr. Haversham so I peeked into his office.

"They were arguing, not yelling or anything, but mad just the same. Mr. Haversham took my tote bag and sweater from the coat tree in his office and practically threw them into my face. He told me to lock up and go on home even though it was half an hour until closing time."

"What did the other man look like?" Tucker didn't know if Maggie's story was significant, but it was the man's unexpected appearance that had made Haversham nervous enough to try to get the plans out of the studio with Maggie. Evidently he trusted her not to open anything that didn't belong to her, and no doubt planned to retrieve them as soon as possible.

"Let me think. He was middle-aged, late forties or early fifties. Medium height, a little on the beefy side. He had light brown hair, thinning on top. I remember thinking he looked like my principal in high school."

"Not exactly the all-time definitive portrait, Maggie. It could fit hundreds of men. Try to think of something else."

"Well, he was tired looking." She glanced at Tucker, who was leaning forward impatiently. Of course, how had she forgotten the obvious? "The birthmark!"

"Birthmark? What kind of birthmark?"

"You know, one of those strawberry things."

Tucker's stomach suddenly felt as though it were filled with molten lead. He knew her answer even before he asked the question. "Where was the mark, Maggie?"

She tapped her forehead. "Just outside the hairline on the right, no, the left side. He must have been self-conscious about it because he jammed his hat on his head when he saw me."

Tucker had never known such a sinking feeling. "That would be a brown felt number with a kelly green band?"

Maggie's eyes widened in amazement. "That's right. But ıow did you know that?"

Of necessity, they spent the rest of the day inside. They ›layed Scrabble, but Tucker's mind was not on the game so Maggie quit, telling him he was no contest. Next they tried ;in rummy, but again Tucker wasn't concentrating and Maggie took every hand.

"Gin," she said dispiritedly as she laid down the winning cards. "You don't really want to play cards, do you, Tucker?"

He gathered up the deck and shuffled it absently. "Not 'eally."

"Then why don't you tell me what it is that's upset you so nuch? It has something to do with what I said this morn- ng. Who's the man in the hat?"

Tucker's troubled glance met Maggie's concerned one. "I :an hardly believe it. I'm afraid if I tell you, if I voice the vords, then it will be true. And God, I don't want it to be rue."

"What?"

"I think my boss might be mixed up in this somehow."

"Your boss. You mean Mr. . . ?"

"Peterson."

"Was that Peterson I saw in the studio that day?"

"I don't know any other beefy, balding guys with straw- ›erry marks and brown hats that it could be."

"But maybe he was investigating," Maggie suggested ıopefully. "You said the department had been watching Haversham for a couple of weeks."

"That's another thing. Peterson assigned a rookie to Haversham. Baker and I got you. Does that make sense? I nean, we've got years of experience. Why would he assign ıs to someone who was obviously not involved and give the ıew guy the ex-con? Evidently he didn't want us picking up on anything."

"Are you saying that Peterson was purposefully trying to botch the investigation?"

"Looks that way."

"And you think he's the one who set those weasels on our trail? Because I saw him at the studio and could identify him?" Maggie's mind had been schooled in armchair mystery solving and raced with possibilities. She'd read too many crime novels not to reach some conclusions on her own.

"It would account for how they kept finding us. There was no bug planted in the car. Peterson was forwarding our location every time I checked in."

"What would have happened if they had caught up with us?" Maggie asked timidly. Her imagination had already given her the one answer she didn't want to hear.

Tucker looked at her steadily. "As hard as it is for me to believe about Sam, my hunch is that we would have been silenced."

"Silenced? You mean iced? Deep-sixed? Wasted?"

He grinned, not thinking he could under the circumstances. "Where did you learn terms like that?"

"I told you, I read a lot."

"Oh, yeah, I keep forgetting."

"Tucker?" Maggie asked after a few moments of silence.

"Hmm?"

"You've had suspicions all along, haven't you? That's why you told Baker not to let on where we were."

He shook his head and pinched the bridge of his nose with his thumb and forefinger. "I thought someone in the department might be involved. I honestly didn't suspect Sam."

"What are you going to do?"

"As soon as this rain lets up I'm going over to Cappy's and call John. I'll tell him what I've found out and ask him to come and get us. It's time to go home and get this mess settled."

"It'll be hard, won't it?"

"What?"

"Accusing Sam Peterson. I know you've always respected him." Tucker had told Maggie about his superior's failed marriage, and how bad he had felt for the man.

"Sam's a good man. If he is involved in this thing, then it's because he went a little crazy when Betty left him. The Sam I know would never get mixed up with crooks like Skirby and Haversham. Why, he's spent a third of his life bringing guys like that to justice."

"Maybe you're wrong about him, Tucker." Maggie laid a hand gently on his arm.

He buried his face in his hands. "I hope so."

Maggie decided to stay at the beach house and tidy up while Tucker went to Cappy's to make his call. They would be going soon and she wanted to leave everything in better condition than when they'd arrived. Tucker had long since reglazed the pane he'd broken in the door, and Maggie had restocked the foodstuffs they had consumed.

As she washed dishes and put them away, she thought about what their leaving would mean. Tucker hadn't allowed her to get close to him since that night on the veranda. At first she had been hurt, certain that he didn't truly care about her at all. Then, as the days went by and she realized what was happening, she had gained some understanding.

If he had not cared, he would have taken, without remorse, what she had so blatantly offered him that night. He avoided her because he had to, because if he didn't he might say or do something to encourage her and they'd be right back in square one.

She loved him. And she was beginning to think that in his own perverse way he loved her a little, too. He was just too muleheaded to admit it. That much she had figured out. But why was he denying the obvious? That's what she had to know before she could decide what to do next.

Time was running out. In a few days they would be home and she would lose what tenuous hold she had over him. He would once more become J. P. Tucker, dedicated Secret Service agent and confirmed bachelor. She would go back to being plain Maggie Ryan who lived life vicariously through the adventures of fictional people like Clementine Kent.

No. She could never be the same again. She could never be satisfied with less than everything life had to offer. The time she'd spent with Tucker had awakened more than just her sleeping sexuality, it had made her aware of everything she had missed. She was no longer afraid of life, no longer too timid to take what she wanted, no longer uncertain.

For some reason, known only to whomever plots the master plan, she wanted J. P. Tucker. And she would have him.

Tucker struck out for the beach house through the gathering gloom of evening. The air blowing in from the north had a definite bite and he hunched deeper into his jacket. His talk with John Baker had been most enlightening. It seemed his suspicions fitted precisely with some his partner had formed as a result of his own investigations.

It was imperative that Tucker get back to D.C. as soon as possible. Luckily Baker had the day off tomorrow and had offered to drive down in the morning to get them. On the way back they could discuss what they had discovered and see what pieces fell into place. There were still too many unanswered questions to Tucker's liking, but once he was back, once he could examine the damning evidence clearly, he felt sure they could resolve the case.

One more unresolved problem was Maggie. She still wasn't entirely safe, not as long as any of those men were on the loose. He didn't want to believe Sam Peterson would go so far as to order them to harm her, but Sam was obviously desperate and Tucker could take no chances with her life. She was too important to him.

That thought struck him like a bolt of lightning. Maggie *was* important to him. Perhaps he even loved her, but what did he know of love? Aside from Pap, who had ever really cared about him? He'd never considered himself particularly lovable, and his experiences with women had reinforced that notion. They'd always been willing to take of his body, to find their ease in his bed, but never had one wanted to be a part of his life.

What was wrong with him that women gave him such a wide emotional berth? He didn't have an accurate roll call, but that many women couldn't be wrong. J. P. Tucker was not husband material.

And yet he sensed that it wouldn't be impossible. He'd seen John and his wife together and envied their closeness and affection. He'd played with their young daughter and longed for a child of his own. He'd often observed the little family interacting and had imagined himself at the head of a table, his wife and children gathered around him.

But he knew nothing about that kind of life. It had been just him and Pap for so long that he wasn't sure how the dynamics of family life worked. He'd never had a father, hardly had a mother. Pap had been a good provider and had taught him those nebulous qualities necessary for manhood, but Tucker had learned nothing about being a husband and father.

He kicked a shell out of his path. Was it too late? He was an intelligent human being; surely he could overcome his past and learn to be all the things a woman like Maggie would want him to be.

Or could he?

When he entered the front door Maggie was coming out of her bedroom. His heart raced at the sight of her. He couldn't bear the thought of losing this woman, but he didn't know what to do or say to prevent it.

She stopped, her hand on the doorknob behind her. "Did you talk to Baker?"

"Yes."

"What did he say?"

"He agrees that we need to get back to D.C. right away."

She was afraid of that. "When?"

"Tomorrow." And tomorrow was only a day away.

"So soon?" She wasn't ready for this interlude to end yet. She hadn't done or said the things to make Tucker care. She hadn't told him how much she loved him.

"He's off tomorrow and said he would leave early in the morning. It's a long drive. I appreciate him taking the time to come."

"Of course."

They stood looking at each other for long moments. Each was afraid to take the first step toward the other. If one of them had extended a hand, smiled the right smile, nodded in encouragement, they might have rushed into each other's arms and discovered how things really were. But they didn't. They couldn't.

"The place looks nice," Tucker commented, looking around the room.

"I cleaned up so Mark and his wife wouldn't find a mess the next time they come down."

"That was thoughtful."

"It was the least I could do."

"Well, just so you won't have to mess up any more dishes, why don't we go into the village and have dinner tonight? Celebrate getting out of here."

Getting out of here was no call for celebration in Maggie's opinion. She felt more like wearing a black arm band. "Okay."

"Do you want to change or anything?" Tucker knew she didn't have a limitless wardrobe—she'd been wearing Mark's wife's summer clothes—but she usually managed to pull something together.

"Sure. I'll be ready in twenty minutes." Maggie slipped back into her room and eased the door shut.

Tucker liked it better when she slammed it. He liked the spitfire Maggie much better than the passive one. Her ordeal had brought out strengths he never would have guessed she possessed during those first two weeks when he had watched her every move.

Maggie Ryan was a woman to grow old with, a woman who would never cease to amaze and delight. She could be a calm, reflective pool one minute and then surprise and exhilarate like unexpected white-water rapids. He had never expected to meet anyone like her, had never known that such a woman might exist. Now that he did, his life would never be the same. She would forever be the yardstick by which he would measure every woman he met.

Maggie slipped the soft jade green fabric over her head and looked in the mirror. The dress was as beautiful on as it had been when she'd coveted it in the shop window in the village. It was handmade. The yoke was intricately crocheted, with the delicate handwork extending to form loose, bell-shaped sleeves. The full-cut bodice was gathered at the waist, and the crocheted hem of the skirt whispered around her calves. She felt truly feminine for the first time in ages as she slipped her feet into the bare little sandals she had found to go with the dress.

She didn't have any jewelry but decided that any adornment would only detract from the dress. She brushed out her long blond hair and freshened her lipstick. She hoped Mark's wife wouldn't mind that she had snitched a quick spray from the cologne on the dresser. It was for a good cause.

She was as nervous as an adolescent on her first date when she entered the living room. Tucker was sitting on the couch, his long legs stretched out before him. He jumped to his feet when she appeared, and she could tell by the appreciative gleam in his eyes that her efforts had not been in vain.

He whistled long and low, reflexively admiring her beauty. "What a knockout you are. Where did you get that dress?"

"I bartered some of my sketches for it. A lady at the little shop in the village saw me drawing on the beach one day and asked me to bring some of my work in. She liked it and I liked the dress." She held out the full skirt and pirouetted in the middle of the floor. "We struck a bargain."

"I'm impressed." He was more than impressed. He was devastated by her charms as well as her ingenuity. Maggie Ryan was not a ragtag little urchin who needed his dubious protection. She was a beautiful woman who deserved the best life had to offer.

"Well," she said nervously. "Are you ready?"

He took her arm and they strolled along the beach to say goodbye to Cappy before walking the short distance to the restaurant in the village. It was well-known locally for its seafood cuisine, and Maggie ordered the she-crab soup and lobster. Tucker pointedly avoided shellfish and selected broccoli soup and red snapper.

As though they had a tacit agreement, both avoided mentioning their imminent departure and they talked only of trivial matters. They were nearly through dinner when a group of locals set up on the little bandstand and began tuning instruments.

"Sounds like we're in for some music," Tucker noted unnecessarily.

"Sounds like it. Do you like to dance?"

"Dance?" He looked as if he'd never heard the concept mentioned in polite company.

"Yes, silly. Dance. Do you like to?"

He'd never thought about it one way or another. He'd danced when it was unavoidable, but found that he wasn't really au courant with the modern steps. That's what he got for letting his grandfather teach him the rudiments. "My fox-trot isn't half bad." Remembering the night at Tingle's he added, "I thought *you* didn't like to dance."

Maggie smiled enigmatically and pyramided her fingers on the table. "We'll see about that."

Again Tucker was struck by her beauty. Her eyes sparkled like emeralds in the reflected light of the candle on the table. How had he ever thought this woman was a mouse? How could he have been so blind to her striking appearance and graceful demeanor? She wasn't a woman many would fail to notice—a realization confirmed by the admiring glances sent her way all night by the other men in the room. He was proud to be with her.

She was a standout, was Maggie Ryan.

After endless false starts the little band bounced into a rousing version of a 1940s classic. "Oh, 'In the Mood.'" Maggie laughed. "They're going to play swing music. I just love it."

"Aren't you a little young to remember Miller and Goodman?" Tucker teased.

"They were my father's favorites. He has all their old records. He taught me to dance to 'Moonlight Serenade' and 'Pennsylvania 6-5000.' Come on," she urged.

"But there's no one else on the floor," he protested.

"All the better. We'll have it to ourselves."

Reluctantly Tucker allowed Maggie to guide him onto the tiny dance floor. He soon began to wonder if he would have the endurance to keep up with her.

"Who'd you say you studied with? Fred Astaire or Gene Kelly?" Tucker was breathless as he caught her to him after a particularly vigorous spin. She just smiled and boogie-woogied around the floor, holding Tucker in thrall by her skillful maneuvers. No wonder she hadn't danced that night at the club, he decided. She would have put them all to shame.

He was lucky and the next number was "A String of Pearls." At least she was willing to slow her pace. "Why,

Mr. G-man," she teased, "I do believe your heart is pounding."

"No joke." He pulled her to him and savored the soft feel of her in his arms. He was sorry their time together was coming to an end because he was going to miss her. He was going to miss her a lot.

Maggie glided effortlessly around the floor, Tucker barely managing to avoid waltzing into the other couples they had lured into action. She closed her eyes and concentrated on the ageless music and the man who held her. She felt as light as an airborne feather, and it was easy to eliminate the rest of the world from her thoughts, to wish reality away, to imagine the dance lasting forever. While she was in Tucker's arms she could pretend they were just two people in love, with a lifetime of tomorrows ahead of them.

She couldn't think about tomorrow. She couldn't think about the sojourn ending and Tucker walking out of her life. A growing sense of panic and fatalism made Maggie certain that would happen. Tucker was so stubborn that he didn't know a good thing when it walked up and kissed him.

She decided to try one more time.

"What was that for?" he whispered after the lingering kiss.

"Does it have to be for anything? Maybe I just felt like doing it."

"In that case, let me know when any more of those urges come over you."

"Don't worry," she assured him as the band segued into "Chattanooga Choo Choo" and she twirled away from him. "You'll be the first to know."

After several dances, Tucker collapsed in his chair and Maggie excused herself to have a whispered conference with the bandleader. There were nods and smiles all around before the leader stepped up to the microphone. "Ladies and gentlemen. One of our guests has requested a song, and since it really needs the vocals to do it justice, she has kindly consented to sing for us. Miss Maggie Ryan."

She grinned and winked at Tucker as the musicians struck up the opening chords of a familiar song. She launched into "Boogie Woogie Bugle Boy" in a sexy, untrained contralto. Tucker stared in amazement as she executed the complicated lyrics as effortlessly as though she were reciting a simple nursery rhyme. She did a commendable job of keeping the tempo and he suspected that with a little more rehearsal she would be outstanding.

Maggie wasn't sure why she had consented to the bandleader's suggestion that she accompany them. She knew the song. She had learned it at her father's knee while he played the melody on his aged saxophone. Maybe she had agreed because it brought memories flooding back and made her feel close to her family.

Since she was feeling unusually uninhibited tonight, and this might very well be her last chance, Maggie had decided it wouldn't hurt to show off a bit for Tucker's benefit. She was gratified to see his mouth hanging open. Maybe he'd get it through that thick head of his that she had more than one hidden talent.

The song ended to thunderous applause accompanied by catcalls of approval. Maggie was suddenly embarrassed and took the chair opposite Tucker with a sheepish grin on her face.

Pride of possession filled him. This wonderful, surprising, beautiful woman could be his. All he had to do was ask.

Too bad he couldn't do that.

Maggie was winded by her unaccustomed exertion. "Whew. That was work."

He leaned across the table and said quietly, "You're just full of surprises, aren't you, Legs?"

She smiled a mysterious smile. "You ain't seen nothin' yet."

Chapter Ten

His moment of truth or what?

Tucker watched as Maggie swirled around the room, holding out her skirts, swaying seductively and humming the haunting refrain of "Strangers in the Night." They'd left the lights off, but Maggie had lit some of the emergency candles and their flickering flames bathed the room in a golden glow. He leaned against the wall of the beach house as if his back had been plastered there along with the wallpaper.

As he watched her, he realized that he had never wanted anyone more. The Maggie he'd seen tonight was not the same scared little mouse he'd shoved out of that warehouse window. Had she changed, or had he? Certainly he'd come to admire and appreciate her as he never had another woman. But there was more to it than that. She dipped and twirled, her secret smile promising things she had no business promising.

He fought back the unwanted feelings and tried to make them into thoughts. If he could think, he could figure out what was happening to him. But he couldn't think and he couldn't act. He could only stand there, glued to the wall.

Abruptly she stopped and held her arms out invitingly. "I don't want the evening to end yet. Dance with me, Tucker."

That would be fatal. He shook his head, but he was a man who took chances. He wanted to touch her so badly that he ached. So he peeled away from the wall and took her in his arms. He pulled her close, crushing her against him, reveling in the feel of her breasts firm and full against his chest.

Maggie's senses were full of this man who could rob her of every thought but him. Tucker's hands spanned her waist, then reached lower to press her more firmly against him. Their thighs strained to touch and their breath came in gasps of long-suppressed desire.

Taking one of her hands from around his neck and holding it in his, Tucker speeded up the tempo of their dance, the melody echoing silently in their minds. His voice was raspy when he murmured, "Ginger and Fred will now do their famous spin, then execute a dip. Are you ready?"

Maggie smiled into his eyes. "As ready as I'll ever be."

They began to hum again, loudly for effect, as Tucker twirled her around, then lowered her dramatically. He held her tightly, but Maggie's nimble feet tangled with his and they landed, laughing, with a plop on the couch. He managed to break their fall but still lay atop her.

She giggled. "You did that on purpose."

He laughed and she felt the vibration clear to her knees. "Nope, I didn't think of it."

Their gazes fastened for a moment and their smiling faces sobered. He looked down at her and was once again assailed by the protective instincts that crowded around him. This was no longer business. It had ceased being so a long time ago, only he had been too stupid to realize it. No matter how hard he fought that strange feeling of possessiveness and that other one that he was too dizzy to put a name to, they were still there. And they were consuming him.

Tucker didn't want to want Maggie. She was breathing deeply, her eyes wide open, her pupils dilated and smoky, staring into his. The feel and sight of her lying beneath him conjured up a fantasy he'd been experiencing over and over for the past few nights. In his wildest dreams she would . . .

"Maggie," he whispered.

"Yes." She wanted to give herself to him now. He was the man she adored with her whole being, and he wanted her. He needed her and she needed him. She wanted him to have her heart, her body and her love.

She caught the tender look on his face as she smiled up at him, and he allowed her to pull his face close to hers. "Oh, Tucker. I wish . . ." Her words melted and whatever she was about to wish for was forgotten. The sudden silence was hypnotic. Her gaze drifted over his face, searching for a clue to what he was feeling.

"What do you wish?" he prompted. He would personally try to make each of her wishes come true.

"I wish you would kiss me."

Why did she have to make it so easy? "I want to. But I don't think I should. It wouldn't be fair to you, and I'm trying very hard to do the right thing." He groaned. "You make it so difficult."

"Do you always do the right thing?"

"Hardly ever," he admitted in a hesitant whisper, his eyes burning feverishly into hers.

"Then don't start now," she breathed against his lips as their mouths met.

He was drowning in sensation, going down for the count. But Tucker didn't care. As ridiculous as it seemed, he felt as if he'd been waiting for this kiss all his life. As if it was his destiny to be forever lost in her touch.

He was floating. Nothing else existed. There was only this kiss, only her lips against his. There was no such thing as protective custody, no such thing as right or wrong. There was only her mouth making love to his, only her body pressed warmly against him. Only Maggie.

Moaning with the ecstasy of her triumph, Maggie turned her body to his, relishing the sensuality that surged within her. He grew taut and hard against her, and when she outlined the rim of his ear with her finger, Tucker groaned as if in pain. Exulting in his evident pleasure and breathing raggedly, Maggie tore her lips from his. She murmured against his ear, "This isn't enough, you know. It isn't enough."

"I know," he moaned, his voice husky with desire.

"I want you, Tucker."

"I know that, too." He held his breath as she arched against him. If he took what she was offering, he knew that he'd never be able to live without her. And that scared the daylights out of him. "Have you forgotten that we leave tomorrow?" He asked the question softly, wishing he could forget it for just a little while.

"No," she whispered. She hadn't forgotten, and neither had he. Apparently he was still looking for excuses, reasons to avoid the commitment she so wanted from him. Why were they doing this to each other, why were they prolonging the agony?

"Shall I kiss you goodbye, Maggie?" he asked, so close that his nose touched hers.

"I'll take what I can get," she murmured as his lips brushed hers. Her moment of triumph was short-lived. Tucker had fought their attraction all along and he was ready to claim his victory. It didn't matter what he *wanted*, his mind would always rule his heart.

His large hand held her face gently as he pulled her to him. Maggie lost the last of her rationality with the soul-shattering kiss, giving herself freely to the moment. His mouth covered hers passionately and she trembled. She had waited forever for this man. How could she lose him now?

His lips were hot and hard as his tongue took possession of her mouth. She luxuriated in the feel of his hard muscles against her soft, straining body as the two of them burrowed into the sofa cushions. Her eyelids closed heavily, and she opened her mouth to him.

Tucker sighed deeply as his tongue probed the sweet warmth within. How had he managed to survive the past several days, or for that matter his lifetime, without her touch? He leaned into her. It was sheer heaven to be close to Maggie, he'd never felt so safe, so secure, yet so exhilarated. It was a rare, novel feeling.

Her hands roamed his back, smoothing the cotton of his shirt against his skin, caressing every ridge of muscle. His hands followed suit but he was frustrated by the clothing separating him from her warm skin. He pressed closer, his voice gravelly when he said, "You're so sweet. You taste so good." His lips investigated the tender hollow at the base of her throat.

"Mmm, you too," she answered, stringing a trail of nibbling little kisses along the curve of his jaw.

Tucker had never felt so alive. But a niggling little voice asked him how he was going to feel when she left and took a chunk of his heart with her. He knew that someday she would leave him. Women always left the men they claimed to love. And Maggie had never even professed undying love for him. She had not claimed to love him at all—not that he would believe her if she did.

But right now, while her willing, pliant body sang out for him, he didn't care. What he felt for her was enough.

He became a slave to his senses, to all that Maggie could make him feel. With her, Tucker felt special, wanted, and he reveled in the feelings that no woman had ever before evoked.

Maggie was stunned by emotions so strong that they took her breath away. She wanted to give herself up to the divine madness that was upon her, to lose herself completely in Tucker, but a rational part of her fought for voice.

This was their last night. There was no tomorrow of forced togetherness to give him second thoughts, to make him stop before they both reached the flash point. If Tucker took her tonight it was because tomorrow she would be out of his life for good.

Reason and sanity returned with a sickening force. If she was going to lose him, wouldn't it be better to live her life unaware of the pleasure and fulfillment she would be missing?

Maggie placed one hand over his to still the delicious tremors he was causing; she pushed his chest with the other. "Stop, Tucker," she pleaded in an uncertain voice.

He couldn't believe what he was hearing. "Why?" he moaned. He could think of no earthly reason to end such pleasure.

"We have to." Maggie sat up and scooted away from him, finger-combing her hair and straightening her dress. Her lips felt heated and swollen, and the fire of his kisses still burned.

He made a strangled sound in his throat, and for a moment he looked stunned, as though she had slammed him in the solar plexus. Then a strange look of wishful longing crossed his strong, lean features. His dark eyes drifted slowly over her face, but the vulnerable expression that wrapped its tentacles around her heart only flickered briefly before his face closed up stubbornly.

"I don't understand, Maggie. You've been giving me the green light ever since that first night. Now all of a sudden, it's no go. Why did you stop?" he asked with as much wonder as irritation.

"Hell's bells, Tucker. This is where we always stop. Every time you take me in your arms, I think, 'Hey, this is it.' But just before you reach the point of no return you draw back, refusing to go further. It didn't look as if you intended to play by your self-imposed rules tonight, so I decided to do it for you." Liar, a voice screamed inside her heart. Just tell me you love me, that's all I need to hear, she pleaded silently.

They glared at each other in stony silence while he let her words sink in. Then his eyes narrowed. "So you decided to pay me back. Is that it?"

"Not exactly. But payback is hell, huh?" she said tightly. He couldn't say he loved her, she realized, because it wasn't true. She studied his features carefully in the candlelight, taking in the white line of tension etched around his sensuous mouth, his flaring nostrils. A powerful emotion played across his face, and with a sinking feeling Maggie realized that it was—anger.

"What are you trying to do to me? Are you mad because I didn't make love to you last week? Or last night? Well, I was ready tonight, even against my better judgment."

He watched the fury explode in her jade eyes and remembered that they'd been much the same color when she'd melted in his arms a moment before. "So? Should that make me happy?"

Tucker rolled his eyes to the ceiling. "I'm tired of all the game playing, Maggie. I'm glad we're leaving tomorrow; maybe I can get my life back to normal. You're the most infuriating female I've ever known. I never know what to do or say around you. Nothing ever goes the way it's supposed to."

Maggie gritted her teeth. Damn him, all she wanted was a little word. All she wanted was to know he loved her. "Go to hell, Tucker."

"I think I just did," he muttered emphatically as he sent her a look heavy with regret. "Living here with you the past two weeks has been nothing but torture." He didn't add that it was exquisite just the same.

"I don't believe it. I don't believe you!" Maggie exclaimed heatedly. "You're finally going to get me off your hands. You never let me forget that I was no more than a troublesome assignment for you, that you couldn't compromise your scruples enough to let yourself love me, even on a temporary basis. But tonight—" She jumped to her feet and paced the length of the room.

"What about tonight?"

"Just how far did you intend to go tonight, Tucker? Since this is the last night we'll spend together, had you planned to let me have my way with you at last?" she asked sarcastically.

With deliberation, he gave her an intimidating look that would have sent the old Maggie scurrying back to her mouse hole. But she stood her ground, defying him to deny her words.

"I thought..." He paused then quickly added, "I really hadn't planned anything at all." Secretly he wondered if perhaps her suggestion hadn't been planted in his mind all along. It would certainly explain his uncharacteristic behavior.

"You're a one-nighter. God knows you've pounded that into my head time after time. No matter how special you make me feel when you touch me, I refuse to be just another notch on your belt."

Tucker rubbed the back of his neck. "Okay. I can respect that. I don't know what was going through my mind since, frankly, my mind hasn't been operating normally since I first met you." He frowned at her in consternation. "Every night I lie in bed and think about you and whatever it is that happens between us. What happens inside me. I lie there wishing it would go away, but it doesn't. It gets stronger every day."

Maggie stared with openmouthed surprise. "Then what is it with you? Or should I ask, what is wrong with me?"

"There's absolutely nothing wrong with you, dammit. It's me. You're driving me insane. I don't want to need you, Maggie. Can you understand that? Can you accept it?"

"Yes. And no."

Their gazes locked and held. Tucker saw his own anguish reflected in the green pools of Maggie's eyes. How could he ask her to accept something that he was finding impossible to allow?"

Maggie's heart went out to him. She could see the pleading look that silently beseeched her to understand and let it go. But every time he touched her or smiled in that special way, the world slid into oblivion. How would she ever get through the days to come? An empty future stretched tauntingly before her, and she wasn't at all sure she could let go so easily.

"Maybe I did think we could give in to the feelings tonight," he said uncertainly. "I don't know." Then Tucker's words echoed her own thoughts. "Maybe I just wasn't ready to let you go." She was audacious and unique and impertinent. But only to himself could he admit that he was totally fascinated by her. "Perhaps if we made love tonight, we'd find that the attraction between us—"

Maggie clapped her hands over her ears. "Please don't say it, Tucker. It's more than a physical longing and you know it."

He ran his hands over his eyes. "It's time to call it a night. We need to go to our separate rooms and come out fighting in the morning. That's what we usually do, isn't it?" Tucker had worked long and hard to erect his protective barriers, but he could feel the fruit of his labor crumbling. If he allowed her to storm the weakened walls, she might just topple them all like a child's building blocks. Then where would he be?

Maggie Ryan was trying to wedge her way into his life, trying to get under his skin and into his very soul. He had always lived by his own Golden Rule: reject first, lest you be rejected.

"We're wrong for each other, Maggie," he said resignedly.

"Keep telling yourself that and maybe in a hundred years you'll believe it." Any anger she felt was gone, replaced by a feeling of utter desolation.

Tucker could think of no response. He was so confused that he no longer knew what was believable and what was not. She might be right for him, but in his heart he knew he was the wrong man for her. He didn't trust women. He couldn't. Maybe he'd come close to it with Maggie Ryan, but she deserved much more than that.

"I'm sorry," he muttered at last.

"Me too." Maggie turned away from him and left the room. He watched her go, and noticed that once again she didn't slam her door. He would have felt better about the whole incident if she had reacted angrily instead of reverting to her old passivity. All the words left unsaid, all the promises left unmade, all the love that would never be hung heavily in the silence.

He slumped on the sofa and watched the dripping candles burn down to nothing. The room was cold in Maggie's absence, and Tucker remembered Pirdy Lee's homemade remedy for "long cold nights." He smiled sardonically. This was sure to be one of those nights, no doubt the first of many to come. With Maggie and all she had to offer him just a wall away, what better time for the artificial warmth of that honey dew?

He couldn't quell his self-recriminations, couldn't silence their reproachfulness. But he could take the coward's way out and turn a deafened ear to them.

Maggie tossed and turned in her empty bed, thinking of the things she might have said. If she had known what to do, maybe she and Tucker would be tossing and turning together in this bed and they wouldn't be wasting their last precious hours alone and miserable. But if they had spent their last hours together, would tomorrow be a beginning or still just the end?

Every night the doors had closed between them, physically and emotionally. He could bring her passions roaring to the blazing point with a simple caress. Then, just before it was too late to stop, he drew back and left her wanting. Wanting all he wouldn't give her.

He claimed it was for her own good. Hah! Shouldn't she be the judge of what was good for Maggie Ryan? She was twenty-five and a virgin, having chosen to remain one until she fell in love.

Well, she was in love now. And she was still a virgin because the man she loved didn't want her. A spark of anger flickered, and she wondered if someone as spunky as Clementine Kent would take this lying down. Smiling to herself, Maggie realized that lying down was exactly the way Ms. Kent would take it. But first, she would march in there and put her cards on the table.

Maggie sat up in bed, relief flooding through her. It felt good to have a plan of action. She would go in there and firmly tell J. P. Whatever-his-name-was Tucker that she wanted him to be the first man to make love to her, and she wouldn't take no for an answer. She wouldn't mention that he'd also be the last. He didn't need to know that.

Holding that thought because it gave her courage, Maggie swept into the living room where Tucker sprawled on the floor, lying across the afghan he'd pulled from the sofa.

"Tucker!" she demanded.

"What?" He scrambled to sit up, and the action made his head spin. His eyes wouldn't get her into focus. "What?" he repeated.

"Did I wake you?"

"No. You okay? Whatsa matter?" The white lightning had rendered his tongue too thick for his mouth.

"Nothing." She plopped down beside him, noticing the jug of moonshine. She picked it up and groaned at its half-empty state. Glancing from the jug to the weaving Tucker, she hoped it wasn't too late to accomplish her mission.

"Thas good." He slumped wearily against the couch. "For a moment I thought something had happened and you needed me."

Maggie steeled herself. "Something *has* happened and I *do* need you, Tucker."

He sat up with difficulty. "Don't play with words, Maggie. I'm in no condition to understand riddles." He grabbed her hand and placed her palm on his chest to prove the point. "My heart is racing and I can't be held accountable."

"It's really pounding, all right," she confirmed, trying not to smile. She was almost too late. He'd been into Pirdy Lee's painkiller and was well on his way to unconsciousness.

"I guess it's reliable—it can take a licking and keep on ticking." He giggled uncharacteristically. "Go on. Laugh at me. But you've been messing around in here," he accused, patting his chest in the general vicinity of his heart. "And you've been messing around in here, too." This time he tried to tap his temple.

"I'm sorry," she lied. "I didn't mean to."

"Sure you did. All women mean to. That's what they do. They get inside a man and become vital to him. Make him unable to function properly without them. Then . . ." He waved his arm in a wild circle above his head. "Pfft."

"Pfft?"

"Yeah, pfft. They're gone. They disappear like cotton candy in a rainstorm and leave him with a hole in his heart as big as, as . . ." He appeared to be thinking. "Big, anyway. I've seen it happen. Lotsa times."

"Not all women are the same, Tucker. You can depend on some of us."

"Not me. Nosirree. I don't want to be dependent on a woman." He laughed bitterly. "My mother taught me better than that."

"Your mother was a very young girl and she made a mistake. A mistake she's had to live with all these years, one she'll be paying for for the rest of her life."

"That's right, defend her. You girls hafta stick together."

Maggie shook her head sadly. "You're wrong this time, Tucker."

"Immaterial." He waved away her protest as if it were a pesky fly. "I've got to get you out of my mind. You're messing up my life."

"How am I doing that, Tucker?" Maggie ignored the sting of guilt she felt at questioning him when his defenses were down. But she loved him, and all was fair in love.

"I think about you all the time. It's all your fault. You're so damned cute and lovable that I don't even care if I never go back to D.C. When I'm with you I couldn't care less about the case, the department, and the whole damned government." He looked at her beseechingly. "Isn't that terrible?"

"Yes. Terrible." She studied him for a moment. He was being more honest and open than he'd ever been before, and she sent a silent thank-you to Pirdy Lee and his truth serum. He *does* care, she thought deliriously. He really cares.

"I've got to get you out of my mind. You can see that, can't you?" He sighed deeply. "I've got to do it so I can get on with my life the way it used to be."

Not if she could help it, Maggie vowed. "Just how do you plan to do that?"

"I don't know." He reached out, gently touching her cheek. "The very feel of your skin is so exciting. It makes me lose all control." His lips brushed hers gently, then he jerked away. "Oh, Maggie, you're doing it again."

"That's right. You might as well get used to the idea."

"But . . . I can't."

"Shut up, Tucker. Don't you want to make love to me?"

"Ever since that first night when I locked you to the bed in those handcuffs. It was so damned kinky."

She smiled. "I was thinking. Maybe the problem is that you have unrealistic expectations. Maybe if you actually made love to me, the experience would be so disappointing that you'd get over me and be done with it."

He considered that seriously for a moment. "Might work." He wrapped her in his arms and her body molded against his until he could feel her pulse points against his. Even in his alcoholic fog, he realized that her thin cotton nightshirt would afford her scant protection from his searching hands.

"I'm crazy with wanting you." He kissed his way from her cheek to her earlobe, then ran his tongue around the rim of her ear.

"You sure have a strange way of showing it." Maggie's nipples tingled against the thin material, and her blood pounded in her veins.

"The only strange thing is that we've waited so long. I want to have you completely," he whispered breathlessly into her ear. "I want to feel your softness absorb me."

Maggie trembled as he surged against her. "I want that, too." She kissed his hair. "Make me know what I've been waiting for. Now." This was it. This was the moment she had waited for all her life. This *was* her life. Any trailing doubts or fears fell during the assault on her senses. She felt his lips on her breast and every touch brought a new and urgent pleasure. Her body arched against his and Tucker groaned from deep in his throat. His hands lovingly stroked her until Maggie sighed with contentment. The sigh became a moan when he slid his hand into the waist of her panties.

"Are you sure, Maggie?" Tucker's senses were reeling but he didn't know if the heady sensations were caused by Maggie or Pirdy Lee's contribution to the distillers' art.

"Stop asking silly questions, Tucker," she commanded, kissing his jaw. "I want you to be the first. I want you to make me a part of you. I want you."

Tucker would have answered, but his words got sucked into the echo chamber that was his brain. His hands no longer seemed a part of him, they forgot what they were doing. Tucker could sense the black wave coming because he heard its distant roar. His last coherent thought before it capsized his good intentions was *Damn, not now!*

Maggie watched in righteous indignation as Tucker's limp body wilted and slipped from her embrace. Enraged that fate could be so cruel, she clutched his shirtfront and wept. "That tears it!" she yelled into the silence. "Damn you, J. P. Tucker, for taking the coward's way out. I'll get you for this!"

The peacefully slumbering Tucker spurred Maggie to further action. For the first time in her life she understood the saying about the fury of a woman scorned. She would not go back to her room and let him off the hook so easily. Their very future might depend on what she did in the next few minutes.

Making a sudden decision, she dispatched his shirt with a few violent tugs, then turned her attention to his other garments, making equally short work of them. Breathing heavily from exertion and from the sight of so much non-threatening masculinity, Maggie paused briefly to steel her nerves.

Could she go through with this plan? Could she feign a rapture that hadn't transpired and deceive the man she loved? Could she stoop so low as to use the man's sense of honor against him? Tucker unwittingly decided his own fate by discharging, at precisely that moment, a contented snore so loud that it could be heard all the way to Kill Devil Hills.

Satisfied that the flagrante delicto scene had been properly set, and mollified that revenge would be hers, Maggie settled down for the longest night of her life.

Chapter Eleven

Hangover? Brain surgery?

Yes, Tucker decided, that was it. An army of tiny, unskilled aliens had invaded his skull and were attempting brain surgery with miniature jackhammers. He would've opened his eyes, but the pain only increased when he tried. He left them closed, uneager to greet the light and suffer further.

His mouth was dry and tasted of dirty socks. He hurt all over more than anywhere else. Every bone in his body screamed in protest when he tried to move from the hard floor where he must have spent the entire night.

It was cold, he realized, but there was a toasty warmth nearby. He flung out his arm to collect the warmth and curled his body into the heat. His hand encountered something soft and silky. Eyes still tightly closed, he patted experimentally, then stopped abruptly when his hand came to rest on a mound of what he could only presume was female flesh.

"Tell me it isn't so," he implored. Ignoring the pain, Tucker forced his eyelids apart. It *was* Maggie. A very sleep-rumpled, pink-cheeked, delicious-looking Maggie. Her eyes fluttered open and she smiled adoringly at him. It was a smile that said she had just spent the most glorious night of her life.

His heart thudded in his chest and he moaned.

Maggie played a quick tug-of-war game with her conscience. He looked so disconcerted, so vulnerable, so... racked with pain. But his discomfort was nothing compared to what he had made her endure, and she decided to play it by ear. "Good morning, Tucker," she said languorously.

"Umm...hi." He mumbled his greeting as he drew away from her, ever mindful of the state of nature he couldn't remember achieving. He closed his eyes, unable to look at her. How could he face her when he could not recall what had happened? Nothing had happened. Had it?

"Look, Maggie, about last night...I don't seem to recall..." His words trailed away. Suddenly she looked so hurt. From her expression, he was certain that what he hadn't wanted to happen had indeed taken place. He'd denied himself for weeks, wanting her more than he'd ever wanted any woman.

Last night had been the highlight of his life and he'd missed it! How could that be? Damn Pirdy Lee's moonshine for robbing him of the joy of Maggie.

"Oh, Maggie," he sighed.

"Don't apologize, Tucker. I couldn't bear it." It was no use, she decided. Revenge didn't taste quite as sweet as she'd thought it would. She had harbored a secret hope that when he woke up next to her all his reservations about commitment would be magically swept away. But here they lay, side by side, their bodies only inches apart, his wall of defenses still firmly erected.

"Do I need to apologize, Maggie?"

"No." He was making her angry, giving her a spoonful of sugar for her taste of revenge.

"Did I...I mean did we...uh..." A warm flush crept up his neck and choked off his words.

"I'm not the kind of girl who kisses and tells," she answered cryptically.

Tucker's heart stopped. "I'm sure I'd remember if we'd made love, Maggie," he bluffed.

She called it. "Do you?"

"Did we?"

There were three sharp raps on the door and Maggie turned to face him. "It must be your partner," she said, sitting up and pulling the cover around her. "I'm sure you'll excuse me while I slip into something a little less comfortable."

"You are not leaving this room until you tell me the truth!" he bellowed, hanging on to his portion of the afghan. "Nothing happened. Right?"

Maggie stood up brazenly and gathered her clothes. Looking levelly into his tormented eyes, she said, "Right." But the way she said it raised even more questions. "Are you satisfied?"

He was anything but satisfied—that was why he was holding on to the cover so desperately. "No." He winced and massaged his temples. "My head is killing me."

"Poor baby," Maggie said with mock sympathy. "That's what you get for floating around up there in moonshine heaven."

The knocker set to with new zealousness, and each pound on the door made Tucker's head throb painfully. "Save your lecture and just open the damned door."

"Open it yourself, G-man." Maggie flounced off to her room to get dressed.

Later, when her meager belongings were once again packed into a brown paper bag on the car seat beside her, Maggie watched the beach house slip beyond the curve and out of sight. Not even her longing could keep it in view, so she sighed and turned to face the front seat and the road ahead. It was the road that would take her back to Sallyville and out of Tucker's life.

She had been introduced to Tucker's partner, John Baker, and liked the sandy-haired man immediately. If he was tuned in to the tension between his passengers he pointedly avoided commenting on it. Instead he and Tucker discussed the case and he was able to give them some good news.

The men who had kidnapped Maggie had been picked up the night before and taken into custody. They seemed not only willing but eager to talk, and so far had given invaluable evidence. Baker liked Tucker's theory regarding the missing plans because, so far, nothing had turned up, and their informants on the street had nothing to report.

"What about Sam?" Tucker asked.

"When I confronted him, he admitted his role in the whole stinking mess. Seems he had a buddy who had twenty-five years with the Department of Engraving. The guy got a raw deal on his retirement so he heisted the plans before heading for Mexico. He and Sam worked out a deal where he could get his revenge and Sam could solve his cash-flow problem. Sam set him up with Skirby and they got Haversham to smuggle the plans back into the country.

"Haversham was supposed to do the engraving, and it was going to be a four-way split, with Skirby and Sam's buddy handling distribution. Sam was supposed to make sure no hot-shot department investigators spoiled the fun."

"It's hard to believe. I guess I'll understand more when Sam makes his deposition. Are the Mexican authorities cooperating in extraditing Skirby and the other guy?"

"The wheels have been set in motion, but it may take a while," Baker complained.

Maggie closed her eyes and leaned back against the seat. The men's murmuring voices drifted around her, but she no longer wanted to hear what they were saying. Tucker was back in his element now, and she was just so much extra, unnecessary baggage. Her role in the all-important case had been played out and she was no longer on his mind.

There were so many things she wanted to say to him, so many truths and half-truths and outright fabrications that needed to be clarified. But he was absorbed by what Baker was telling him and had no thoughts for her. And even if he were willing to listen, how could she bare her soul before an audience? She would just have to bide her time and hope that she got him alone soon.

Self-preservation was his only hope.

Tucker had dumped Maggie on her doorstep like so much toxic waste, anxious to be free of her reproachful looks. In the two weeks since they'd left the beach house he hadn't seen her even once. He hadn't so much as talked to her on the phone. He knew his behavior was inexcusable, but a man had a right to protect his emotional well-being, didn't he?

He'd convinced himself that what he thought had happened that night, never had. He almost believed that he didn't owe Maggie Ryan a thing. Except to get out of her life so she could get back to her search for her ideal man, the art lover who enjoyed strolls in the park.

Today's meeting had been unavoidable. Maggie had been subpoenaed in the government's case against Peterson, Haversham, Skirby and associates. Her testimony had been crucial in obtaining an indictment since no counterfeiting charges could be filed. No money had been printed, the plates hadn't even been completed, so convictions on conspiracy and kidnapping were the best they could hope for.

When he saw her at the preliminary hearing his heart constricted with a joyous pain. She was strong, speaking up in a clear, no-nonsense voice. She was the picture of credibility, and no one had been surprised when the suspects were bound over for trial.

After his own testimony, Tucker left the courtroom with only a quick glance in Maggie's direction. His plan was to leave and never look back, but during the moment when their eyes met and held, he was lost. His sense of honor would not let him leave without at least trying to explain why he hadn't contacted her.

She would be coming out of the courthouse any minute, and when Tucker wasn't checking his watch, he kept his eyes glued on the entrance.

Maggie had to keep reminding herself that she was an adult with a duty to perform. It had been difficult to keep the tears at bay when she'd testified and identified her assailants, but she hoped Tucker had been proud of her. He avoided her eyes during the long-drawn-out testimonies and only once, at the end, had he looked her way. She had tried to send him a silent message but she wasn't sure he had received it.

The past two weeks had been torture for Maggie. When she had cried on Holly's shoulder about the injustice of it all, her friend had not been very sympathetic. According to Holly, things had a way of working out for the best. Wasn't her new notoriety making her an overnight sensation in the art world? Maggie wasn't sure that she wanted her sculptures to sell because she had been an unwitting accomplice in a counterfeiting ring, but Holly said she should be glad they were selling for any reason.

Then Holly came up with a sure cure for the depression that weighed on Maggie. She took her on a wild shopping spree in D.C.

Maggie liked the new clothes she had purchased and felt they enhanced the newfound confidence she had acquired. She was on her own for the first time in her life and she loved it. She no longer needed to waste her time in a meanngless job just to pay the rent; the sale of her art would cover her expenses for quite a while. She was doing what she had always wanted, so why wasn't she happy? Because, she told herself, she would never have the one thing she needed to make her world complete—the love of J. P. Tucker.

"Hey, Legs," called the heart-stoppingly familiar voice. "Wait up!"

Taking a deep breath and forcing a smile to her lips, Maggie turned. A few feet and insurmountable differences separated them, but still their gazes met and locked. "Hello, Tucker."

"How have you been?" he asked softly, longing to feel her in his arms just one more time.

"Okay." The word scraped her throat.

He smiled, and it would have taken her breath away if she hadn't been holding it, suspecting just such a trick.

"I've been reading about you in the papers." He wished Pap hadn't raised such an honorable man, so he could have avoided this painful encounter.

"I've read about you, too." Maggie searched his dark eyes for a glimmer of hope but could find none. "I understand you've been given a promotion."

"Yeah, I guess the department was fed up with all the bad press Peterson's duplicity gave them, so they issued that press release about my dedication. It wouldn't have looked good if they hadn't given me a promotion to go with it."

How like him to underplay his role. "You'll always be a hero to me."

When she grinned, his heart turned over; he didn't deserve a word of praise from her. "Thanks," he mumbled. "I hear congratulations are in order for you. You've created quite a stir in the art world. Even Baker, clod that he is, owns one of your sculptures. He has it in a place of honor on his mantel and brags to anyone willing to listen that he knows the artist."

"I've gotten a lot of requests from the gallery for more work. I've alerted my family and they're shipping other pieces from storage back home. I'm having a show at a prestigious gallery the first of the year."

"I guess things couldn't have worked out any better for you," he said quietly.

"No," she murmured. "I guess not." Not when I'm in love with such a pigheaded fool, she added silently.

"I guess you'll be rich and famous in no time."

"I'd settle for being happy and fulfilled," she said wistfully.

"That'll come, too, Maggie. Someday." There was something different about her, and it took several moments for him to realize that she was wearing some artistically applied makeup. He didn't like it. Without it she had been beautiful in a natural way. With it, she looked like a cover girl.

Tucker glanced at the stylish suit and smart coat she wore. What had happened to her baggy sweaters and shapeless skirts? She seemed even taller in her high-heeled shoes, and he wondered why she'd given up sensible pumps.

Neither Tucker nor Maggie realized how far they had walked until they came to the entrance to a small park. Possessively, he took her arm and steered her inside.

"I thought you might like to walk in the park," he explained as though he'd known all along where they were headed.

Maggie buttoned her coat against the November chill. "I thought you didn't like walks in the park. Too dangerous, wasn't it?"

"Nothing seems dangerous since I've met you. Besides, it's broad daylight, what could happen?"

She might fall even more deeply in love with him, Maggie thought. "I'd rather not walk too far in these shoes."

"I was going to mention that. What's with the new look?"

"Part of my new image," she said as she twirled around. "What do you think?"

"Devastating." And calculated to make it damned near impossible for him to tell her he wouldn't be seeing her again.

What little hope Maggie held tightly in her heart began to die. She could almost hear his thoughts, she was so attuned to him. The bad vibrations were nearly tangible, and she knew he was going to tell her to forget about him, to get on with her life. She knew it as surely as if she had written the script.

"Been on any interesting stakeouts lately?" she asked nonchalantly.

He grinned, recalling their escapade, and she saw a trace of that old devilish twinkle in his eyes. "No, but then anything would seem tame in comparison to tailing you."

Tucker liked talking to Maggie, had nearly forgotten how comfortable he felt with her. She refused to let him take himself too seriously, and he felt lighthearted around her. It was almost as if the emotional backpack he'd been toting around forever had finally been lifted from his shoulders. "I'm taking a leave of absence."

"Why? Is something wrong with your grandfather?"

"No, he's fine. I just feel like getting away. My work hasn't seemed too rewarding since I've been back. I've even been thinking about quitting the department." That much he hadn't even admitted to his best friend, Baker.

No. He'd just told his best friend.

"Don't do anything rash. Take your time and make the decision that's right for you, Tucker."

"I guess all this business with Peterson has given me second thoughts. I used to have a lot of high ideals. I wanted to right the wrongs of the world. That's a laugh."

"There's nothing wrong with having ideals."

"Sam Peterson used to say that I reminded him of himself when he first started. I don't want to wind up as disillusioned as he was."

"Sam made some mistakes and he'll pay for them. But you should feel comforted that the day I saw him at Haversham's studio, he was trying to call off the counterfeiting deal."

"Just because he got cold feet doesn't make up for what he did," Tucker pointed out.

"No, maybe not."

"I can never forgive Sam. After all, it was because of him that Haversham put the plans in your purse and nearly got you killed."

"I couldn't help feeling a little sorry for him after hearing his testimony. We don't know what was going through his head, so we can't condemn him. In fact, I think we owe him our gratitude."

"Why should we be grateful to Sam Peterson?" Tucker asked with disgust.

"If he hadn't assigned you to follow me, and hadn't set those hired thugs on our trail, we'd never have met. We wouldn't have had those two weeks together, and I might never have seen the ocean or gotten the chance to sing with a band." And her life wouldn't have been irrevocably changed forever.

"But Sam was so different when I first met him. I was always so impressed with his high ideals and vision."

Maggie shook her head sadly. "People change."

"It was his marriage falling apart that did it to him. When Betty left him after twenty-six years, it destroyed him."

"As tragic as that is, Tucker, people get divorced every day without resorting to a life of crime."

Maggie was getting suspicious. She knew he was trying to convince himself and her that marriage always turned out wrong. It was just more ammunition in his war against commitment.

Tucker disregarded her comment. "Sam and Betty had been married half their lives. You'd think that was a sure thing."

"I guess there are no sure things."

"No, and that's pretty damned frightening. Lately I've even found myself wondering about John and his wife, if they're really as happy as they seem. Maybe it's just an act they put on for company."

"That's ridiculous, Tucker. Maybe there aren't any guarantees, but people have to learn to live and love and laugh together, how to keep communication open. Not all marriages turn sour."

Tucker shrugged noncommittally. "Any relationship is like betting on a horse race. Pap always says, 'If you can't afford to lose it, don't bet it.' I agree with him."

"I think he was talking about money, Tucker. Not emotions."

"The stakes are even higher when you're wagering your heart."

Maggie looked at his determined jaw and knew that he meant everything he said, that he would never give an inch. "You have a unique way of looking at things, Tucker. Sometimes you just have to take a chance. If you don't, nothing is sure to happen. Do you want to live with that emptiness?"

Clearly he'd made up his mind not to love her or let her love him, and this was his hardheaded way of letting her down easily. Maggie despaired that he would ever come to his senses and realize they belonged together.

The sad look on Maggie's face wrenched Tucker's heart. "I know what you're thinking," he accused. "You think this is all a line I've come up with to convince myself that we're wrong for each other."

"Is that what I was thinking, Tucker?" Her tone was soft and sad.

"Come on, Maggie. I know you and I know how your mind works. You think I'm using this as an excuse not to let myself be in love with you, don't you?" he insisted.

Was he searching for reasons to deny his feelings, she wondered. The fact that he was looking for excuses was suddenly encouraging. Maybe it meant that he had already fallen.

Maggie sat on a nearby bench, stalling for time to digest this latest development. Tucker followed and sat down beside her.

"That *is* what you're thinking," he bluffed.

"Not really," she snapped. "But who am I to say what I'm thinking? We both know you're the mind-reading authority."

"Don't get cute. We spent a lot of time alone and I think I know you pretty well. In fact, I probably know you better than anyone." He sounded surprised, as though that notion was a revelation to him, as well. He wouldn't look at her, staring instead at a couple of young children playing on the grass with their mother.

It was an ordeal for Maggie to remain outwardly calm when her anger was like a sensitive explosive—ready to detonate at any moment. She should have known they would come to this and avoided any contact with Tucker at all. He roused her either to passion or fury; there didn't seem to be much middle ground in their relationship.

"You're so damned single-minded, Tucker, that you make me want to scream. If you're waiting for me to justify your blockheaded theories of romance, forget it! And quit putting words in my mouth and thoughts in my head. You're too scared to admit that those are your own conclusions, not mine." She turned away from him, folded her arms across her chest and followed his gaze to the romping children.

Watching the mother with her children, Maggie found herself full of envy. The young woman, not much older than

Maggie herself, looked on fondly, maternal pride glowing in her face.

Suddenly, a large dog came bounding toward the babies in pursuit of a tossed ball. Alarmed, Maggie gasped and jumped to her feet. "Watch out!" she called to the little family. Even as she spoke the words, it was too late. The clumsy, yipping dog knocked over one of the little ones and the child sat down hard on his well-padded bottom, howling his indignation.

Maggie stiffly took her seat, watching as the mother knelt to console the small boy. The woman wiped and kissed the tear-streaked face and smiled reassuringly at her son before calling the dog over to them. If it were possible for an animal to look contrite, it did. It took some coaxing, but the child finally giggled and stroked the dog, eventually allowing it to swipe at his face with its long pink tongue.

Maggie sighed. "Smart lady. She made sure the little boy knew that the dog was really friendly and hadn't meant him harm."

"What if it had bitten him? The poor kid might have ended up needing rabies shots. If I was the child, I don't think I'd have been too eager to take the chance."

"The boy's mother must have seen the dog playing around all the children in the park. He hadn't bitten any of them and she knew it. The little boy knew he could trust his mother to keep him safe."

A two-year-old child had learned something that Tucker never had. To trust in another person's love enough to take risks. Maggie was amazed at how such a simple incident had illuminated so much for her. He didn't believe in his own innate lovableness, and he never would if it made him vulnerable to the possibility of pain.

Maggie had always taken love for granted. Her family had lavished it on her so generously all her life that she saw it as her due, an inalienable right like freedom of speech. Never before had she understood the power of love to shape personalities, to change the course of lives.

Tucker's eyes met hers and lingered until a rush of memories overwhelmed him. Memories of holding Maggie, kissing her, feeling secure in her willingness to share herself with him. Of their own accord, his fingers reached out and touched her lips, tracing their fullness. "May I kiss you goodbye, Maggie?" He gently wiped the lone tear that trembled down her cheek.

His touch ignited powerful feelings in Maggie. Not again, she begged him. There had been too many goodbyes already, and she wasn't sure she could put up a brave front in the face of yet another one. "I couldn't bear it if you did," she whispered sadly.

"I know. I'm sorry, Maggie. I never meant to hurt you."

It was finally over. Maggie tried to accept it, knowing that this was her last chance to leave with her dignity intact. She would let him go because he wanted to go, and even though she knew it took more love to lose him than it did to fight for him, a final desperation seized her. He could go, but she wanted to give him something to think about during the days and nights ahead. "I love you, Tucker. But you do what's right for you and don't worry about me." When he just stood there with doubt and indecision on his face, Maggie made a shooing motion. "Go on now, just go away!"

She turned her head away from him and wiped her eyes with the back of her hand. Tucker was motionless as her words burned into his consciousness. "I'm no good for you, Maggie. It just wouldn't work."

She could have hit him. Only Tucker could make her want to kiss him one minute and throttle him the next. She'd become a more assertive person during the time she'd known him, but she curbed her desire for a physical outlet, instead venting her frustration by shouting.

"You're right! It would never work. I'd be totally crazy within a month." Maggie poked a forefinger into his chest, emphasizing each word. "But I love you. And you can deny it until hell freezes over, and it won't change a thing."

Tucker was touched by her words, touched and shaken. "So what's love? All the love in the world and fifty cents will get you a nice cup of coffee."

"I refuse to stand here in the cold and argue with you." She whirled away from him. "You once accused me of having the emotional experience of a fifteen-year-old. True as that was, it still gives me a few years on you. I feel sorry for someone with the emotional handicaps you have to live with."

He spun her back around and fought the impulse to crush her against him. The crisp breeze had coaxed a becoming pink tinge into her cheeks and tossed her long curls around carelessly. "Don't waste any sympathy on me. I'm perfectly happy." He hadn't known he could lie with such a straight face.

"Is that so?"

"Yes."

"So what *are* we standing here for? You've surpassed your normal level of surliness and I'm out of patience."

Hurt and anger swirled around them like dust in a whirlwind. After long telling moments, Tucker cleared his throat. Maggie had seen the bitter expression leave his eyes, only to be replaced by one she couldn't name. "I have to be going," he said finally.

"Yes. You do."

"I'm leaving town today. I'm driving up to Pap's."

You're running away, she wanted to yell at him.

"Good luck with your show, Maggie. I hope everything works out for you." Don't forget me too quickly, he pleaded silently.

"Thanks," she managed. Please leave. Maggie didn't know how much longer she could pretend to be unshattered. "Have a safe trip." She had nearly added that he should give her love to Pap, because she felt as if she knew him. Now she never would.

They backed away, their hands trailing down the other's arm as if reluctant to relinquish the final thread of physical reality. A stiff breeze kicked up and spun the last of the crackling leaves around them like russet autumn confetti.

Maggie's heart was constricted with pain as she watched her life walking away from her. "Have a nice life, Tucker," she murmured.

Chapter Twelve

Well, I can't just kidnap him!"

Maggie paced the floor, wringing her hands. "If he's too dumb to realize what a wonderful thing he's giving up, I can hardly drag him kicking and screaming to the nearest justice of the peace, can I?"

"Why not?" Holly took another cinnamon roll from the bakery sack and pulled up a chair in Maggie's sunny little kitchen.

Maggie slumped down in the chair across the table from her, suddenly drained of the nervous energy that had kept her going for the past two days. "What do you mean, why not? He's gone and there's not a damned thing I can do about it."

Holly shrugged. "Okay. Forget him. There are plenty of men out there and a lot of them are looking for a permanent relationship."

"I don't want any other man," Maggie wailed. "I want J. P. Tucker."

"Then go get him, girl." Holly rolled her eyes as though the idea was too elementary to expound on. "Geeez."

"Get him! Get him? I couldn't even hold him when I had him. What makes you think I can get him?"

Holly poked the rest of the sweet pastry into her mouth and noisily licked her fingers. "You'll think of something."

"How can you sit there stuffing your face when my whole future has just been shot off the map? What kind of friend are you, anyway?"

"A patient one. Look, Maggie, I've listened to you whine about this guy ever since you got back. It's time to stop talking and do something."

"And that is . . . ?"

"From all you've told me, it sounds like the man is nuts about you but has some kind of hang-up about admitting it. So what you do is dust yourself off and keep going back until you wear him down. Unless he's a total drain brain he'll wise up." Holly reached for the bag again. "You want this last roll, Maggie?"

"No, you take it." Maggie couldn't be bothered with food while the fate of her love life hung in the balance. "I told Tucker I loved him, but he claims there's no such thing. How do you suggest I fight that?"

"Do I have to think of everything?" Holly chewed thoughtfully. "Tucker sounds like one of those up-front kind of guys, so maybe you should try the direct approach."

"Like handcuffing myself to his wrist and declaring my undying love?" Maggie asked caustically.

"Now that has its merits, but it might be *too* obvious. Think of something else."

"Tucker's only problem is that he can't trust. He doesn't believe in commitment because he's never allowed himself to risk it. He's thirty-four years old and the notion is entrenched. I don't think there is any way I can overcome that obstacle."

"Okay."

"Okay what?"

"So handle it the way the old Maggie would. Give up." Holly shook her head. "I thought you changed while you were gone, that you were finally going to live your life instead of watching it pass you by."

"I have changed, Holly. But I'm not sure that I wasn't happier when I was an observer. The participation is getting a little wearing."

"Too true," Holly agreed, crumpling the empty bakery sack. "But look how much ground you've gained, how much you've experienced since you decided to live a little."

Maggie grinned. "It wasn't a conscious decision, I assure you." She propped her chin in her hands and tried to think of a plan. Plans always made things look more hopeful than they really were.

She thought back to her comment about handcuffs, and a smile turned up the corners of her mouth. She reached over and tapped Holly lightly on the arm. "You're right. I'm not totally without resources, and I'll be damned if I'm going to stand by and let someone else make decisions that will affect my life forever. Especially when that someone is as big a fool as J. P. Tucker."

Holly perked up and grinned back. "Now that's the new Maggie we all know and love."

"You got that right!" Maggie was suddenly filled with outrageous inspiration. Mentally she bade her fictional counterpart, Clementine Kent, goodbye. As much as she appreciated her alter ego's encouragement, she didn't think she would be requiring Clementine's help in the future. In fact, if things worked out the way she hoped, she wouldn't have much time for reading at all.

Maggie jumped up and ran to her room, determined to follow through before pride and common sense could stop her. Holly stood in the door and observed Maggie's preparations with approval.

"Going cruising for a man, Maggie?" she asked with an impish grin.

Maggie winked audaciously. "You'd better believe it!"

Maggie paced off the fourteen feet of Tucker's cabin for the hundredth time. Good thing the floor was planked with hardwood, she decided, or she would have worn a path by now. Waiting was beginning to wear on her nerves, so she reminded herself that what she was waiting for was worth the vexation—Tucker.

She'd left Sallyville and Holly, her cheering section of one, yesterday afternoon. With the help of a map, she'd located Hanging Rock, the small town where Tucker's grandfather lived. Baker had been most helpful in giving her directions to the house high in the pine-shrouded West Virginia hills and had good-naturedly wished her luck with her quest. She'd taken off with little more than a full tank of gas and a pretty preposterous plan, now that she thought about it.

She'd arrived late and found lodging at a nearby motel, planning to rise early. Knowing Tucker's sleeping habits, she hoped to catch him with his defenses down. Though he hadn't mentioned it, Maggie knew that he probably still harbored some doubts about their last night at the beach house. He couldn't be sure that what she'd led him to believe hadn't actually happened.

With any luck she could appeal to his overworked sense of right and wrong and insist that he marry her since her virtue and reputation had been compromised. Maggie knew that most men would scoff at something as outdated and anachronistic as a shotgun wedding, but she was hoping that Tucker's old-fashioned values would prick his conscience enough to at least allow her to discuss it.

When she arrived with the sun on the elder Tucker's doorstep, Maggie was dismayed to discover that Tucker had not yet arrived. She gained an unexpected supporter in the gentle, white-haired old man who had raised Tucker, and over a hearty breakfast found herself confiding in him.

"J.P. can be mighty obstinate when he sets his hard head on something," he'd told her with a shake of his shaggy head. "Take his mother, for example. For years I've been after him to try to make his peace with her. But the Tuckers have always had a stubborn streak a mile wide, and he just dug his heels in and refused to budge on the matter. I didn't know about you, child, but I guessed that something like an earthquake must have moved him."

"Why is that?"

"'Cause he called me and said he'd be a few days late—he was headed for Norfolk to see Rebecca. That's my girl—J.P.'s ma, you know."

Pap—he'd insisted she call him that—had poured them another round of strong black coffee and they had discussed Maggie's plan of action.

At length the old gentleman had lit his pipe, leaned back in his chair and regarded her seriously. "Do you love him, gal?"

"More than anything in the world."

"Then take what you want, because my boy is too dad-burned fool-headed to be much help in the situation."

"Pap, will you help me?" Maggie feared she was overstepping limits, to ask a grandfather to conspire against the grandson he'd raised from infancy.

The old man took a deep draw on his pipe, rocked his chair down hard and propped his elbows on the table. "Jest you tell me what you want me to do," he'd said with a big grin remarkably like Tucker's.

And that was why she was pacing the floor of the small cabin Tucker had built deep in the woods. According to Pap, it was his thinking place, the spot he returned to whenever he wanted to be alone to work out knotty problems. The old man had instructed her to go there the next morning—Tucker was sure to head for his private place once he'd properly greeted his grandfather.

It was now well past noon and Maggie was growing more nervous by the minute. If he didn't show up soon she would turn tail and run. The more she thought about it, the less Maggie was convinced that the little "surprise" she had arranged for Tucker was such a good idea.

She toyed with the cheap metal handcuffs in her sweater pocket. Only a child's toy she had purchased in the motel souvenir shop, they wouldn't seem very threatening to someone who was used to employing the real thing. Still, they were meant to be symbolic, and serviceability had not been a consideration.

Glancing out the small window in the front of the cabin, Maggie noticed something red moving through the evergreens that lined the narrow trail. She moved in for a better look and was soon rewarded with the sight of Tucker striding toward the cabin. He was dressed in snug-fitting blue jeans and a heavy plaid hunting jacket, the collar turned up against the wind.

Her heart lurched and her pulses quickened. The next few minutes would determine the course of her life. She wiped her damp palms on the legs of her own jeans and tried to arrange her features in a welcoming smile.

Tucker kicked a pinecone out of his path and followed the familiar trail to his refuge. He hoped the solitude would help. God knew, nothing else had. He admitted that he felt better after having talked to his mother. His mother. Funny that in all his years of growing up he hadn't really thought of Rebecca as anyone other than Pap's daughter.

They'd had a long talk that lasted well into the night. His reserve had been weakened by his mother's obvious pleasure in seeing him, and bit by bit, during the night, he'd given up the past. Once he'd let go of the burden of distrust and resentment he'd carried around for so long, the animosities of a lifetime had soon been shed like a smothering cloak.

Rebecca had clutched him to her just the way he had longed for as a child. She'd held him and told him she loved him and begged him to forgive her for all the mistakes she'd made. She'd told him she didn't expect him to forget, but she hoped he would finally give her the chance to make up for lost time. And it felt good to finally gain a mother at the unlikely age of thirty-four.

He was glad he had taken the risk. He'd had a moment of indecision before calling Rebecca, and worried that she might let him down yet again. But when he'd heard her voice on the phone he'd thought of what Maggie had told him about taking a chance on someone's love.

Maggie. She had been right and he owed her a lot. He wished he could talk to her and tell her how wrong he'd been to close up his heart in an airless cell. Now that he'd reclaimed the maternal love that he could have had so long ago, if only he hadn't been so stubborn, he was ready for more.

And more meant Maggie because Tucker could never love any other woman the way he did her. So why was he headed for the cabin and seclusion when he should be high-tailing it back to Sallyville? he asked himself.

Because he had just taken one giant step down the road to commitment and he wasn't sure he was up to another one so soon. Also, he feared that Maggie's feelings for him might have changed since that day he'd turned his back on her in the park. He wouldn't blame her if she never wanted to speak to him again. Could he swallow his pride and call her when he got back to Pap's?

He could. And he would.

He swung open the cabin door and ducked to step inside. It was gloomy, as usual. He should have incorporated more than two small windows into the floor plan, he thought wryly. Once his eyes adjusted to the reduced light, he noticed a silent figure standing quietly in the corner.

"Maggie?"

She stepped toward him. "Tucker."

"Are you really here?" he asked in wonder. He feared that his obsession with her had conjured up her image and she would disappear like smoke on the wind.

"Yes. I'm really here. I've come for you." Maggie tried to walk closer but found her feet would no longer carry her where she wanted to go. She held her breath and prayed that he would not make her resort to the chicanery she'd arranged as a backup.

"What do you mean, you've come for me?"

"Since you are too hardheaded and stubborn to know when you are well off, I've decided to take matters into my own hands." At least she could talk a good game.

"And just what do you propose?" Could that really be why she was here? He folded his arms across his chest to keep from taking her in his arms prematurely.

Maggie was overwhelmed by the urge to fling herself on him. If he tossed her aside, at least she'd have the pleasure of his touch one last time. She fought down the impulse and said with surprising calmness, "Well, actually the proposing was supposed to be your line, but since you never cooperate, I guess it's up to me."

"What's up to you?" Tucker had a good idea where this conversation was headed and was thrilled to be along for the ride.

"Dammit, Tucker, do you have to make everything so hard?" Maggie advanced, and didn't stop until she was knee-to-knee with him. She twined her arms around his neck and looked him in the eyes. The delightfully fresh woodsy scent of him almost made her forget what she had to say. "You have to marry me. I won't take no for an answer."

"I wouldn't want you to—"

"There's a justice of the peace waiting at Pap's cabin," she interrupted. "And if you won't come peaceably I'm prepared to resort to force."

"Very well..."

She pulled the toy handcuffs out of her pocket and dangled them menacingly in front of his nose. "And Pap has a shotgun that he's willing to hold on you until you do the right thing and marry me."

"Pap's sided against me?" he asked with mock incredulity.

"That's right. We can do this the hard way or the easy way—what'll it be?"

Tucker gathered her into the warm circle of his arms and quietly reveled in having her so near again. The green sweater she wore emphasized her flashing emerald eyes, and he knew they were eyes he'd love looking into for the rest of his life. "You know me," he whispered. "I'm easy."

But Maggie was so wound up that she wasn't listening. "I promise you, Tucker, if you don't agree to marry me right now, I'll pursue you like a Mountie. I won't give up until I've got my man—"

The rest of her words were lost as his mouth closed over hers. He'd decided that was the only way to get her attention. She strained against him and a soft little moan escaped her. He felt her arms tighten around his neck when she returned his kiss with equal fervor. There was no doubt in his mind that he was exactly where he was always meant to be.

Maggie tore her lips from his and stared up at the man she loved. "What's it going to be, Tucker? Will you go quietly?"

"No."

"No?" The question fairly trembled on her lips.

"There's something I want to say first."

"What?"

"I love you, Maggie Soon-to-Be-Mrs.-J.-P.-Tucker Ryan. If you hadn't come to me, I would have come to you." His lips brushed hers in a whisper-soft caress.

"Really?" Her eyes filled with tears of joy and her heart overflowed with love. "Does this mean I'll finally find out what J.P. stands for?"

"Nope."

"Why not?" she asked indignantly, stepping back to fix him with a level look.

"Because it doesn't stand for anything. My mother couldn't make up her mind when she named me, so she decided to give me initials and let me make the choice when I grew up."

"May I make a suggestion?" Maggie wriggled closer and wondered if Tucker would be a stickler for conducting the honeymoon *after* the wedding ceremony.

"Be my guest," he invited.

"How about Just Perfect?" she offered innocently.

Tucker's laugh filled the small cabin. "I thought you said there was a man with a shotgun waiting for us."

"He can wait just a little longer, can't he?" she asked, wriggling ever nearer.

"Maggie," he whispered huskily. "If you keep that up, we'll keep the justice of the peace waiting till morning. I want to do this thing right."

"I don't think you could do it wrong if you tried," she murmured.

Tucker allowed his hands to roam where they would for a moment of pleasure. "There's one thing I'd like to get straight before we take our vows."

"Anything," she moaned.

"What about our last night together in the beach house? There seems to be a black hole in my memory, and I had a hangover the next day you wouldn't believe."

"I'd believe it," she said, nibbling on his ear. "I'm the girl you passed out on. Remember?"

"Not really, but I'm damned glad I did. I'd hate to think that you'd saved yourself all those years for—"

Maggie put the tips of her fingers against the flow of his words. "I saved myself for you."

"You're a treasure worth waiting for, Maggie." He kissed her gently. "I'm just sorry you had to come all the way up here. I would have come for you."

Maggie clung to him and pouted, "You mean you would have deprived me of the pursuit?"

"I'd be the last person to ever deprive you of anything, Legs. The only thing you'll be pursuing from now on is happiness."

COMING NEXT MONTH

#508 ONE OF THE FAMILY—Victoria Glenn
Author Alexandra Reynolds was in L.A. under false pretenses—but that wasn't a problem until she met handsome Mark Conover and fell in love. What would he do when he found out why she was *really* there?

#509 TANGLED TRIUMPHS—Terri Herrington
When consumer advocate Reese Cartwright found a flaw in a product, he did everything he could to bring it to public attention. Only this time, the target was a toy manufactured by Carly Abernathy—the woman he'd never stopped loving.

#510 A MIST ON THE MOUNTAIN—Stella Bagwell
Broken Bow Lake was just what the doctor ordered for Dallas attorney Adam Slade—peace, quiet, and fishing guide Jessie Kincaid. Could a city slicker and a country gal find "happily ever after"?

#511 PERFECT PARTNERS—Jennifer Mikels
Meg Gallagher swore she would never get involved with another cop after her fiancé was killed on duty. But that was before Detective Sergeant Ryan Brady arrived in town. Her head told her to slow down, but her heart was full speed ahead.

#512 NO COMPETITION—Debbie Macomber
Shane Reynolds had long admired Carrie Lockett's art—almost as much as the artist herself. But buying her paintings was easier than getting close to Carrie. Could he convince her that together they could create a masterpiece—of love?

#513 ON RESTLESS WINGS—Mia Maxam
The Red Baron had no business landing his plane in Gloria's pasture and disrupting her solitude—or being so handsome. She wished Major Ross Adams would just fly away. . . and take her with him.

AVAILABLE THIS MONTH:

#502 IT TAKES A THIEF
Rita Rainville

#503 A PEARL BEYOND PRICE
Lucy Gordon

#504 IN HOT PURSUIT
Pepper Adams

#505 HIGH RIDER
Olivia Ferrell

#506 HEARTS ON FIRE
Brenda Trent

#507 THE LEOPARD TREE
Valerie Parv